The Ghosts
Guernsey's Past

Kate Sebire

Table Of Contents

Dedication

I would like to thank everybody who helped make this book happen and the islanders of Guernsey who contributed their stories.

Acknowledgements

I am truly grateful to everybody who contributed their fascinating and frightful stories; I owe a great deal of thanks to many individuals.

I would like to thank my boyfriend, Stephen, for supporting and encouraging me throughout the different stages of putting this book together.

Thank you to my family members who were sent on a mission across the island in search of places to take photographs for the book. Thank you for your patience, especially as a couple of places were hard to find, Rachel Blondel, Elicia Upson, Lucy Smart and Beccy Smart.

I would like to thank my three dogs, Rocky, Jack and Cheech, for the constant disruptions, knocked over paperwork, nudging me whilst typing on the laptop, and barking loudly when I was trying to concentrate, I probably would have finished this book a lot quicker, but I got there in the end.

Many thanks to Guernsey Ghost Stories.

About the Author

Kate Sebire was born on the Island of Guernsey in the Channel Islands. She left there aged eighteen to move to London where she still currently lives. Her fascination with the paranormal started from a young age growing up on Guernsey, an island which has so much history, legends, and folklore, stories of witchcraft, ghosts and ghouls, fairies, orbs, and tales of black dogs with red eyes.

She was instantly drawn to finding out more about everything that appears unexplained, which over the years led her to believe that ghosts really do exist and that there is an afterlife.

A couple of years ago she completed her Bachelor of Science (Honours) degree with the Open University covering a range of topics.

She now works in a special educational needs school as a mentor for children with social, emotional and behavioural difficulties, ADHD, learning disabilities etc.

Disclaimer:

The stories that follow have been told by people willing to share their own personal ghost sightings and strange experiences, all names mentioned are real, some people chose to remain anonymous for personal reasons.

Introduction

My fascination with the paranormal first started at an early age. Born and raised on the beautiful Island of Guernsey, one of the Channel Islands' supernatural hotspots, it is not surprising that so many people have experienced paranormal encounters. An island with such a long and rich history of stories passed down by generations of families over the years, of ghosts and ghouls, legends of witchcraft, myths about fairies, ghoulish dogs and various sightings of German soldiers apparitions and other hauntings throughout the island.

These are just a few of the reported terrifying tales in the pages that follow, amongst my own personal ghostly experiences and incidents of true, real-life unexplainable reported cases of paranormal activity told to me by family, friends and other Islanders of Guernsey.

My Family's Ghost Stories:

Like many other families in Guernsey, my own family have seen/experienced things that they can't comprehend. Some members of my family have contributed their own true stories of ghost sightings and other paranormal experiences that have happened to them over the years.

The following personal testimonials from my relatives reveal some intriguing, spooky, and unexplainable ghostly encounters.

My brother Robert has seen various sightings of strange ghostly apparitions throughout the different parishes of Guernsey, with most of the sightings occurring very late at night and also being witnessed by either a friend or family member. All of these people who were there at the time with my brother for these unexplainable encounters have been able to acknowledge and describe identical details after having seen the appearance of a ghost materialise in front of them.

Guernsey Location

Guernsey is the second largest of the Channel Islands, with Jersey being the largest in total. There are seven inhabited islands, including Alderney, Sark, Herm, Jethou and Brecqhou. Guernsey is an island 9 miles in length and 3 miles in width, situated in the English Channel, it is 30 miles from the coast of France and is 75 miles from the south coast of England. With a population of 63,000 (2021 est.) Guernsey is divided into a total of ten parishes. Its capital is St Peter Port which is the main port on the east coast of the island. Guernsey is a British crown dependency with its own government, and it is not part of the UK or the European Union. The traditional native language of Guernsey is Guernnesiais which is also known as Guernsey patois or Guernsey French. Nowadays, English is the official language. The climate in Guernsey is temperate with mild winters and mild, sunny summers. This island is the sunniest in the whole of the British Isles as it is warmed by the adjacent Gulf Stream.

Guernsey Information

The island of Guernsey has such a rich and varied history that dates back thousands of years, with archaeological remains that have been discovered showing early human settlement dating back to 5,000 BC. There are many megalithic sites dotted around the island, such as menhirs, dolmens and a mysterious carved standing stone figure.

Guernsey was also used by the Romans as a trading centre, it is thought that they arrived around 56 AD and stayed for around 250 years. A Romano-Celtic trading vessel, Asterix, was discovered in St Peter Port harbour in 1982. The ship caught fire and sank around 280 AD, the original ship was 22-25 metres long, of which some 17 metres of its lower parts remain. Objects found trapped in the bottom of the ship included roof tiles, pottery from Spain, France, Algeria and, Britain and leftover food was even discovered stuck in the bilge of the ship. Eighty coins were also included in the Roman finds, with the latest dating to after 275 AD.

The Vikings also plundered the Channel Islands, which then came under the control of William Longsword, son of Rollo, the first Duke of Normandy, back in 933. After successful raids, the Vikings began to colonise the Channel Islands, with many places and the names of the islands themselves having Old Norse roots. The name Guernsey is of Viking origin with the second element of Guernsey (-ey), meaning island. The first element is uncertain, traditionally taken to mean green.

Privateering and smuggling were also rife on the island. From 1689 to 1815, the privateers earned Guernsey millions of pounds, with mansions being built on the island from the proceeds seized and plundered from enemy shipping. By early 1800 there were 115 privateers operating out of Guernsey. There were many cellars and vaults full of contraband all over St Peter Port, taken from the cargoes of the ships, smuggled goods, particularly rum, brandy, wine and Chinese tea and silk – Guernsey being the main entrepot for smuggling with England.

Witchcraft features prominently in local folklore on this island. In an 80 year period from 1560 to 1640, forty-four people were burnt at the stake at the bottom of Tower Hill in St Peter Port, and thirty-five were banished from the island for life on suspicion of performing witchcraft in Guernsey. The headland, which is between Perelle and L'Eree, known as the 'Catioroc', was notorious as their main meeting place whereby Friday night ceremonies took place (Le Sabbat des Sorciers). Built into many of the old houses and cottages in the west of the island are pieces of flat granite protruding out of the chimneys known as 'Witches' Seats', according to folklore in the Channel Islands, these small ledges were used by witches to stop and rest on as they flew to their sabbats.

The German occupation of the Channel Islands during World War II lasted from 30th June 1940 until liberation day on 9th May 1945. 23,000 islanders – half of the island's population, which was 42,000 at the time – left Guernsey to mainland England. Many defensive concrete fortifications were constructed around Guernsey's coastline, with many thousands of foreign prisoners and labourers being shipped to the island to complete the construction of German bunkers, tunnels and, gun emplacements. Two days before the occupation of the island on 28th June 1940, three German planes bombed St Peter Port Harbour killing thirty-four people and injuring thirty-three. The attack also saw forty-nine vehicles that were either damaged or destroyed, with the majority of these lorries carrying tomatoes that were waiting to be exported to the British mainland being mistaken for military trucks by the Germans.

Chapter 1: German Soldiers

German Soldier

An old boss I used to work for told me this story. He was driving home one night to his house down L'Eree (St Pierre du Bois) in the lanes when he saw someone on an old-fashioned bike in full German uniform, about 11 pm at night. He was like, "Did I just see that? I mean, who would be dressed as a German soldier on an old bike at that time of night." He said it just passed him down the lane.

-Robert

The Milkmaid and the Soldier

I stayed in a self-catering cottage barn that was in the King's Mills, and one night whilst I was staying there, I saw both a milkmaid and a German soldier in my bedroom. The milkmaid had the wooden frame over her shoulders, and she walked across the room, along the side of my bed and disappeared through the wall at the bottom of the bed! I also awoke to find a German soldier standing behind my head, dressed in uniform and a cap, looking down at me! It was a bit of a shock at the time, but later on, I found a photo of him and his cap in the Occupational Museum.

-Anita

The Hovering Soldier

My ex-husband told me years ago that he and his then-girlfriend saw a German soldier hovering over the lookout area of Fort George, hence a quick exit. This was in the early 80s.

-Alison

Fritz

I had a strange feeling once when I was in the Mirus Battery whilst doing an exercise with Civil protection. It was like someone threw a small stone at my head. One of the Battletec helpers told me it was Fritz the ghost, which most of them had experiences with previously. Apparently, he liked playing tricks on them.

-Julie

Schultz

My mum and dad were staying at a hotel in St Martin's as they were visiting Guernsey, looking to move over there to live. One afternoon, my mum saw that there was a man kneeling, looking out at sea. He looked at my mum and smiled, my mum smiled back and thought what an unusual uniform, she turned to my dad to ask what the uniform was and looked back, and the man had vanished. All weekend she had a name in her head. I can't remember the first name, but the surname was Schultz. She came back to the UK and told us of this man, the uniform, and the name.

Fast forward to us as a family moving to Guernsey, we visited the German Occupational Museum, and there was the same uniform where the collar unclipped off the jacket with the colouring of this certain uniform, meaning that it was from a certain rank in the German Army. There was also a wooden cross with this man's name on it!

We had moved to Fort George and decided to walk to the graveyard. There was a metal plaque with all different names on it, and we noticed that this man's name was also on there. We found his grave, I think, the second row from the front!

-Nikki

Gormer

In the early 60s, my Gran lived along the front in St Peter Port, close to Wyndhams Hotel. Her house was a sort of one room on each floor affair with a staircase running up the side of the house. Every night at 9 pm, starting at the bottom and going up all four flights of stairs in the house and the steep steps into the attic, we would hear heavy booted footsteps. They would stop once in the attic and were never heard at any other time of the day and never went down, only up. I don't know who found out, but somebody told my Gran of a German soldier billeted in there during the war by the name of Gormer who had hung himself one night in the attic. Subsequently, every night at 9 pm, as the footsteps passed the living room level, my Gran would call out, "Goodnight, Gormer!" He never replied, nor did his steps falter at the sound of his name being called.

As a child, I was fascinated by this, it never scared us. It was just very freaky. My Gran and all eight of her children and their spouses and all of us grandkids heard it. You could set your watch by Gormer.

-Kriss

Chilling German Soldier Procession

I grew up at Grandes Rocques (Castel), where I was sat on my windowsill one night having a sneaky cigarette. My room looked directly across to the beach and Grandes Rocques Castle. I saw a line of figures that looked like German soldiers marching in single file. They had a glow around them. They were in the car park where the bus stop was heading up towards the Castle. I was speechless, I just sat and watched until they faded away.

-Anonymous

Chapter 2: Shadows, Mists And White Figures

Spirit Scents

When I moved into my new house, I could smell smoke in one of the rooms. Someone who is a retired firefighter had told me that there was a fire in the property a long-time back with a fatality (I never mentioned to him about the smell, just told him where I moved to). My fur baby won't go in that room, and the TV and radio turn on at night by themselves, too. I have also seen a shadow out of the corner of my eye from time to time, and it felt like someone was sitting by me. I'm not scared, feel threatened or unnerved by the presence, but I am aware that it's there.

-Paula

The Ghost That Followed

One night I was walking back home from the Legion about 12:30 am, and it was pouring down with rain. I had made the same walk by myself plenty of times before, but on this night when I got to the entrance of the road which takes you to the L'Islet dolmen (St Sampson), I suddenly felt different, like something wasn't right. As I walked towards the dolmen, I turned around and saw a white figure over my shoulder, so I started to walk a lot faster, and it followed me.

I freaked out a little bit, so I started running, but it stayed with me from the top of the lane to the exit of the dolmen. I didn't feel threatened in any way, but it was creepy. I just couldn't believe what I had seen.

-Robert

Ghostly White Apparition

One night, sometime after midnight, my mates and I were out in our cars. We had about four people in each car; we decided to pull into the Les Amarreus car park (Vale). As we were side by side parked up in the car park, something tall and white ran across the car park right in front of us. I quickly turned on my car lights, but it just disappeared. It emerged from the beach over the car park towards the park, and it was so quick, whatever this thing was. Three of us saw this white misty figure running. We couldn't believe what we had seen that night.

-Robert

The White Shadow

A few years ago, my daughter Helen and I were walking the dogs one evening on L'Ancresse common (Vale). It was just getting dusk when a white shadow passed across the pathway right in front of us. We both looked at each other, and I ran off and left Helen standing there.

Another time we were driving up the Les Canus road, and the same thing happened again. Something white passed right in front of the car, we both saw it and said, "What was that?" I didn't leave Helen that time, seeing as she was sitting in the front seat while I was driving.

-Jane

The Disappearing Figure

My friend and I one day were doing the reservoir walk (St Saviour) when near the end we stopped at the gate (at the bottom of the track) to take a picture together. We were both looking at the camera, and in the corner of my eye, I saw someone walking down the slope towards us in white!

I looked up at the exact same time as my friend, and the figure disappeared into thin air. She then said to me, "Did you see that person?" and we both said, "In white." There was no one around. Just me, her, and her dog.

-Anonymous

Ghostly Walker

One night, my wife and I were walking our dogs through the lanes near our house in the Vale. We were walking alongside each other, and we both had small torches with us when suddenly I felt like someone was walking up behind me. I turned slightly and saw the outline of a figure behind my left shoulder. I slowed and stepped in behind my wife to allow them to overtake, and no one did, and when I shone my torch. I saw that there was no one there. Neither my wife nor the two dogs were aware of what I had seen, but I am sure that I saw someone.

-Bryan

The Ghostly Mist

I don't know the background in this area, but I was going home around 9:45 pm one night when I saw a person-size white mist on top of the hedge by the Chene traffic lights (coming from Specsavers). As I drove towards the lights, this mist came down off the hedge, crossed the road in front of my car to the corner pavement next to the Chene Hotel and the lane to Petit Bot and just disappeared! It gave me the chills!

-Anonymous

Ghost Rider

One night we saw what looked like a man walking along La Ramee at the side of the road at approximately 11:30 pm when this figure literally just disappeared, there were two of us that saw it, so it wasn't our imagination. It was the end closest to Long Camp, right where all the windy bends start. It was a very strange experience.

The second time that I saw a ghost was about thirty-five years ago. I was a backseat passenger in my dad's car, and my mum was in the front passenger seat. It was a wet stormy night at about 10 pm. We were driving alongside the smelly pond when suddenly a figure appeared in the road. It went over the wall into the pond and disappeared, right on the sharp corner. My dad and I saw it, but my mum did not, even though she was sat in the front seat of the car. We made some enquiries and found out that many years ago somebody had lost their life there on their motorbike on a wet and stormy night.

-Sandie

The Playful Spirit

I am not going to mention the house as such, but this is a story from about three to four years ago. My partner and I were staying in a house at the back of a graveyard, and someone had passed away in the house prior to us moving in. I had always sensed something about the house, and every morning I was there on my own, I had the same recurring realistic dream of the house shaking and the curtains moving, which was very weird. Anyway, one specific night I was on my way to the bathroom when I saw a large human-like misty figure behind the lounge glass door. I didn't tell my partner as it was very dark, and it all felt a bit surreal, so I questioned what I had seen. I thought that I could have just been seeing things.

Later on that evening, my partner went into the kitchen, came back and swore that I was standing behind him and made a coughing noise (I freaked out at this point as I hadn't told him my experience). Then again later on that evening my partner went for a late shower, and suddenly the TV did that awful fuzzy picture with that terrible sound and then went back to the normal channel minutes later. Needless to say, I hid under my covers until he came back. It was no harm at all, but I have a feeling this spirit was playing with us that night, and it's a moment I'll never ever forget.

-Kayleigh

A Glimpse of the Past

One night I was walking through St Jacques estate (St Peter Port) around 8 pm, I think. I was walking through the estate car park and out in the open when I'm pretty sure I saw a white figure walk past me about 5 metres away. It was in old maid-like clothing but 'walked' with a hunchback, it seemed.

-Bailey

Early Morning Fright

It was early one January morning, about 4 am back in 1994, and I had just left work. As usual, I would go for a drive before going home, and this time was with my first car as, before this, I used my parent's car. After my drive, I was on my way home up Valnord Land in St Peter Port. It was still very dark, and as I came up to where the old school used to be, which had just recently been knocked down, I started to slow down to about 10 miles per hour which afterwards I thought was strange as I don't normally go that slow.

As I got to where the entrance is to the old school, I saw that there were two figures standing there in white monk's robes; their heads were facing the ground so I couldn't see their faces. At this time, the hairs on the back of my neck stood up as I felt a cold shiver go through me, and I was gone as fast as my car could get me out of there. I just wondered who would be out at that time of the morning in those clothes. When I was working nights and sometimes had to walk back home along those roads, it was not something that I enjoyed, experiencing weird things and strange feelings in those areas that I never got walking elsewhere at night.

I spoke to someone about it four years later, and they said that someone had told them there is an area from the Rohais and around the Safeway supermarket area along Collings Road that was monastery land, according to some very old

18

Guernsey maps. I saw an old map a few years ago, which confirmed this.

-John Vokes

Chapter 3: Cats, Dogs And Paranormal Activity

The Old Man and His Dog

I was with an ex-girlfriend one night, and we were parked up at Chouet Headland (Vale) at about 3 am in the morning, when we noticed an old man dressed in a long hooded brown cloak walking behind the car with a scruffy looking dog. Suddenly they just vanished into thin air. It really freaked us out, like the way he was dressed. It was so strange. They passed behind us and just disappeared.

-Robert

A Dog's Intuition

This happened in my old house not long after my mum had passed away. I went upstairs with my dog, and she just stared up into the corner of the ceiling above my head and started barking. I couldn't stop her, and she wouldn't take her eyes off the corner of the bedroom ceiling. It was very strange.

-Alex

Purrsonal Experiences

I lived in Pedvin Street (St Peter Port). When it was just me living in the block of three flats, a few strange things happened. My cats would sometimes stare up at the ceiling, and even when I went over to try and distract them, their eyes would stay fixed on the ceiling, and they would stand on their back legs sometimes, still staring at the ceiling.

Another thing that happened around 11 pm almost every night would be where I heard what sounded like a cat running up and down the hallway – the flats are all the same layout, and the hallways are all wooden floors. Also, I know what it sounds like when my cats run up and down my hallway – but on these occasions, I could hear the exact same noises above me. My cats would always be asleep at the time or not moving around, so it wasn't them. All of the windows and doors from outside were closed, so no animals or people could get into the flat above, and nobody lived there at the time that this was happening.

I've always found this very strange, and I know that animals can sometimes sense things that we can't.

-Racheal

A Heavenly Tail

We used to see a shadow wind its way around our top bannister that looked like a cat. I had noticed it a few times, and then I found out that my daughter had, too. As soon as we spoke about it openly, the cat disappeared. It was almost like it just wanted acknowledgement.

-Angela

The Ginger Cat

My dad was in a care home, and every time we went to see him, he would talk about a ginger cat in the room that nobody else could see. One day, he even said that it was sitting on his lap, but there were never any cats in the home. Not long after that, he sadly passed away.

My husband, daughter, and mum went to see the flowers on his grave at the Vale church one afternoon, and as we approached the grave, we noticed that a big ginger cat was sitting on my dad's grave. The cat got up and came up to us. When we left, he went and sat back on my dad's grave.

Since that day, we have never set eyes on him again. If one person had gone, I guess, no one would have believed it, but we were all shocked when we saw that ginger cat sitting on his grave that day.

-Jane

Ghost Dogs

As a child, I remember going through Talbot Valley (St Andrew) with my dog, who ran off chasing butterflies, when suddenly, all around me, I could hear the loud panting of dogs. There were no other dogs around, and mine had vanished. It really freaked me out. Another time I was up there with my mum having a picnic and heard it then too – both of us did. Again, there were no dogs in sight. We packed up hastily and left. I will always remember those incidents back then. Although I haven't really given much thought to it, it was definitely loud dog panting that I heard.

-Anonymous

Ghost Cat

My experience is similar to others regarding a ghost cat on the bed. When I was little, my cat Poppet used to sleep with me every night, and I got my cat called Kenny two years ago (My first cat since Poppet thirty-five years ago). I quite often think that Kenny cat has come to bed as I can feel him walking across the bed, but he's not there. I'll say hello and look over the duvet to stroke him, but there's nothing there.

-Anji

Sensitive Creatures

I was walking my dog at Rouge Rue (St Peter Port) just after 6 o'clock in the morning. No one, nothing else, was around when all of a sudden, my dog started barking and going mad before crying and backing away. I could not get him to walk any farther up the hill. He was having none of it. I had no choice but to turn round and walk back down the hill very quickly. Something certainly spooked him. We have walked it so many times before, and nothing like this has happened. My poor dog could not get out of there fast enough.

-Paula

Purranormal Activity

As a baby, my mum told me that whenever I cried, one of the cats would jump up by my feet, and I would immediately stop crying. This cat died when I was about seven years old but would continue to sleep by my feet many times over the years. After their deaths, I've seen most of my animals, sometimes walking past them and forgetting they have gone. I have also had dreams about them too.

-Anonymous

Ghost Whiskerer

I've had the feeling of a cat jumping on my bed where I could feel the weight up against my side or pressing down on top of me, which both of our last cats used to do when they were alive.

-Martin

A Heavenly Welcome Home

On entering my parents' house with them, we were greeted by doggy paws pattering towards us excitedly in the hallway, except their dog had died a week previously. Both my dad and I heard it, and we just looked at each other in amazement, but my mum packed up and thought that it was funny, she is deaf so couldn't hear anything.

-Vanessa

Tails of the Unexpected

Our first cat still visits our home every now and again, and he passed away eleven years ago. He has jumped on beds, and he has been heard coming in under the gate and walk across the landing. It wasn't our other cat that was heard as he was outside when we heard the other cat. It is quite comforting, really.

There is a ghost of a resident's cat in the care home that I used to work in. He can often be seen either sitting on the windowsill where he lived or walking down the corridor. The cat was always walking around but sadly passed away, followed a few weeks later by its owner. I saw the cat a few times sliding around a corner like it used to tail held high.

-Anonymous

Paw Prints from Heaven

We lost our only dog last year and have since seen wet paw prints in our flat when it's rainy outside, found new dog biscuits in the middle of freshly hoovered rooms, plus we have heard her whine, and we have also seen her rush past us in peripheral sight. We know that she's still with us!

-Rachel

Chapter 4: Spirit Children

Atin

Can imaginary friends be ghosts? When I was about six or seven years old, I lived in a cottage near Le Picquerel (Vale). My parents said I had an imaginary friend called Atin, who I would blame any misbehaviour on. If I got told off, I would say, "But Atin did it!" Some people would say that it is fairly common for children to invent an imaginary friend, but this is a really unusual name to mention coming from Guernsey. Where would I have heard that kind of name being used!

Out of interest, I looked up this name, and it said Atin is a Hindu boy's name and is Hindi originated, with multiple meanings, the great one and strong.

I believe that children can see and interact with spirits, but this ability fades away later in life. I have no recollection of Atin from my childhood years. I wish that I could remember some details from back then as there are admittedly lots of reports of children seeing ghosts or stories of imaginary friends that have turned out to have once been alive.

Unexplainable spiritual encounters reported by children with accurate accounts of people who really existed, whereby such detailed descriptions of the spirit's appearance, old fashioned clothing and names are revealed to their parents often with the child saying that the invisible friend follows them around, gives them advice, talks to them and tells them what to do, possibly causing children to say and do things that would get them into trouble.

Even more extraordinary is when names and locations are checked out by the children's parents, revealing that the names were, in fact, real and the locations were correct.

-Kate

The Crying Children

When I was a little girl, my family lived in the St Stephen schoolhouse. My mum used to hear children crying upstairs, but no one was there as we were outside, playing. The kettle used to go off on its own, and there were other strange goings-on in that house. I was the youngest child and used to go into my parents' room and hiss at them, and I would also talk to them in a different language. I was only five or six, but I remember a recurring dream about an old lady on a rocking chair laughing. It was like I was possessed! But when we left that house and lived down L'Islet, I didn't have these dreams anymore, and I didn't sleepwalk or talk again either, very strange!

-Lyndsey

The Girl in the Dressing Gown

I was sleeping one night when I woke up, and all I could see was a little girl in a dressing gown floating above my bed smiling at me! I stared at her for a few seconds, squeezed my eyes closed because I felt scared. I opened my eyes again, and she was gone.

-Alex

The Vanishing Little Girl

My dad told me this story about a little girl years ago. Going back to when he was in his 20's he saw a little girl in a white dress on his way home from darts very late at night. He said that she was near Summerfield estate (Vale), and he started to follow her as he thought it was a bit late for a girl to be out and about alone at that time of night. She skipped all the way up the road and vanished near the gates to the quarry! A very scary story that he told me, but he remembered it like it was yesterday.

-Kylie

Ghostly Little Visitor

Our little visitor only really started to appear when our boys reached a similar age to what I would say he is. He runs with our boys, and it seems like he enjoys their company. He is not around all year round; his presence normally starts at the end of August and can be felt until about February, then he goes for a while. For a short time, he was a little naughty. He would do stuff like move things, and he had a real thing for turning on the electric toothbrushes inside the bathroom cabinet in the middle of the night. I found talking out loud when I felt he was about to seemed to stop that. I've never been scared of him. When the spirit appears in the house, he is usually seen a lot throughout the daytime and during the morning. He has also been known to appear a lot in the month of December.

-Anonymous

The Humming Ghost Girl

I remember many years ago walking home when I was living in a flat at Sous les Hougues (Vale), I walked near the entrance to the house next to the farmhouse when I saw what appeared to be a little girl walking across the road and enter the gateway. She seemed to be humming. I thought this to be strange as it was about 12:30 at night. I had a good look into the front garden, but there was nothing there.

-Paul

It Follows

I used to live in a house at Rue au Pretre Rectory Hill (Castel) back in the '80s. It was 5:00 o'clock in the morning, and my husband had got up and gone downstairs to make a coffee before going out to work. I heard him shout to me to come down, but I was half asleep, so I just turned over and went back to sleep. The next thing I know, he's waking me up in a panic. He started shouting, "There's a girl at the bottom of the stairs." I replied, "There can't be. The doors are still locked. No one could possibly have got in." He went back down to see if she was still there and shouted up, "She's gone."

I never saw her but started to get really bad shivers and shake a lot when I was in the house on my own. This happened so much that I went to the doctor to see if I had any strange illness. But he put it down to panic attacks and gave me some kind of relaxers. This helped, until one night myself and my husband were sat down watching TV when all of a sudden, the light switched itself off. My husband got up, thinking that the bulb had blown. Hence, he took the bulb out and replaced it. The strange thing was the switch was in the 'off' position. When he went to turn it off, that's how he realised it was not a blown bulb. Very freaky.

I don't know if ghosts follow people from one house to another, but the house I live in now also has its own ghost. I have a picture of it on my phone. It's a full apparition of a lady. I wonder if this could be the same ghost that has followed from the old house!

-Linda

The Face at the Window

I lived with my mother, brother, and grandfather in a big flat on Mill Street (St Peter Port) and had to climb up a hundred steps to get to the flat. One day I saw a young girl looking out at me through a window inside the flat. As I was on my way in, I did a double-take. She was gone. Lots of other stuff happened up there. Lights turning on and off in the long hallways and in the nighttime, it never felt safe. When I was in bed, it always felt like something was looking at me. I used to cry all the time because I was scared. I was around eight or nine years old at the time, and I hated living there.

-Mandy

The Giggling Ghost Girl

Ghosts have a sense of humour, too, you know. Well, one of the two that share my current house does anyway. One of them just wafts about the place, making us cold, but the other one described by my daughter as a 'funny dressed girl' and glimpsed by me, as maybe being nine or ten years old, dressed in Victorian or earlier fashion clothing, with a white apron over a black dress. My wife burns incense around the house to try and get rid of the ghosts, but the girl puts the incense sticks out and then giggles. Every time you hear the giggle, then check the incense stick, sure enough, it's been put out. This is then followed by a smell that I can only describe as resembling the Old Spice aftershave, it isn't, but that's the nearest I can get to it. I can't get a good look at her. She is only glimpsed out of the corner of the eye.

-Kriss

Wandering Spirit

My hubby and I both saw a little girl standing in our bedroom one evening. I told her to go to bed as I thought she was my daughter being naughty, but she walked straight through the door without opening it. It did not scare us for some reason. I told my neighbour a few doors away the next day, and she told me that she and her husband had also seen her the same night. I think that she was looking for someone, we have not seen her since, so I hope that she found who she was looking for.

-Anonymous

The Little Chimney Sweep Boy and the Lady

I used to live in a house with my ex-husband and my children in Victoria Road (St Peter Port). That house was haunted, but I was never scared. The kettle used to boil on its own, the back door to the garden would open on its own, I would also get knocking sounds on my lounge door at night time. So one night, I decided to open the door to see what was causing this noise when I saw a little chimney sweep boy dressed in rags sitting on the stairs. There was nothing scary about him, so this didn't frighten me. There would also be lots of banging noises in the house, and my children would tell me about a lady that lived under the eaves in the cupboard who would go into their rooms and check in on them at night and sometimes she had a little boy with her.

I found out that the house was one-hundred-and-fifty years old. It must have been a massive house years ago as there were two doorways blocked off by walls that would have led to the house next door, my kitchen had a cast iron fireplace, and there were two tall fireplaces in the lounge and bedroom areas, we had the old sash windows and huge under eaves cupboards. I really liked living there and would love to know the history of that place. I didn't get any horrible feelings living there in that house. In fact, it was quite comforting.

-Anonymous

Ghost Girl

I must have been about thirteen or fourteen years old, and it was the summer holidays. I was with my friend Lyndsey walking back from the beach. We decided to take a shortcut back through the Vale church graveyard. As we were walking down from the church, we saw a girl walking down the footpath entrance from the main road.

We thought that it was a girl we knew called Emma, so we shouted out her name a couple of times, but she didn't look towards us, which we thought was a bit strange, as even if it weren't Emma who we thought it was walking down the path usually if someone is shouting out, most people would look over in that direction. Still, she just carried on walking with her head down.

I remember the girl was wearing a black and white top with a swirled pattern on it. We could only see the top half of the girl as she walked down the path behind the low wall towards our direction. Seeing as we didn't get a response, we decided to run down the hill to go and say hi as she was still walking down the pathway towards the graveyard.

But when we got to the bottom of the hill where it meets the pathway, the girl had just disappeared. Lyndsey and I looked at each other to say, "Where is she?" There is nowhere she could have gone. It was like she had just vanished into thin air.

-Kate

Lyndsey's Comments:

I remember that day so clearly. It was very strange and like you said there was nowhere for her to have gone! She just disappeared. It freaked me out for ages.

The Boy Who Disappeared

So, I usually walked to work, but this day was a little drizzly, and I guess I must have been running a little late, so I decided to drive in. It must have been around 7:40 am, as I was always at work by 7:50 am at the latest. I drove down past the Elizabeth College towards the pedestrian crossing on St Julian's Avenue (St Peter Port) at the junction with Candie Gardens. The lights changed to red, and I stopped. There were no cars ahead of me, so my view was completely clear.

I looked to the left side of the crossing, and there were two men and a young boy waiting to cross. I remember distinctly that one man had a brightly coloured shirt and the other a suit. The boy looked around eight years old and was wearing a grey school uniform, shorts, a grey blazer, a shirt and tie, and a school cap. As the three individuals started crossing the road, I watched them. Then as the two men reached the other side, I realised I hadn't seen the boy get to the pavement. He just seemed to vanish! I looked back at the left side just in case I had missed him going back there. No, nothing. I kept looking back and forth, and a car behind me beeped. The lights had changed, but I hadn't noticed.

That strange feeling you get in your stomach and head when something is wrong came over me, and I carried on to work repeating to myself, "What did I just see!" There was no way that he could have got to the other side of the road without seeing him. The two men were walking far enough apart that he couldn't have been hidden from my sight. Whenever I think about it now, the hairs on my arms stick up, and I wonder who he was and why I saw him that day.

-Kelly

Dream of the Dead

I have lived in my house for three years, but I've never felt or seen anything strange over the years. Then, suddenly, on a few different weekends where my two young children, aged four and one, had been playing outside in the garden, I saw a little girl running through my kitchen into the hall or poking her head around the doors. My husband has seen her too. The girl is around six or seven years old, and one night I dreamt that she spoke to me and told me that her name is Megan, and showed me a photograph of her with her parents (I did not recognise them). I don't feel anything strange in the house, and I'm not scared or anything. I just think it's odd that it's just started to happen. This little girl doesn't look like she is from years ago. She looks like she would come from our generation. She wears a pink dress and has blonde/brownish hair just past her shoulders.

I've only seen her on a Sunday afternoon over two weekends and one night in my dream. My children were always running between rooms, so maybe I didn't always notice her. I asked my daughter, who's going to be two, if she sees a little girl, and she nodded. I asked where she is. She pointed outside to the playhouse and said, "In house." My husband then asked if she plays with the girl, and she nodded again and said, "Play nice." The little girl seems to be around more often recently, during the evenings and through the night. My husband said he swears she was whispering to him when he was trying to sleep, but he couldn't hear her properly and was quite freaked out.

One day we had been outside working in the front garden. It was around 9:00 pm when I took my son upstairs to bed. My husband said that he saw the little girl kind of run up after we had gone upstairs. Another time I went to bed on my side of the bed looked as if someone had slept in it. I had made the bed in the morning, but the covers had been pulled back, and there was a head dent in the pillow. It wouldn't have been my son as he goes to bed and doesn't budge, and my daughter sleeps in a cot.

The little girl seems very happy and playful, running around and likes to play peekaboo. I did think that she seemed a bit sad in my dream, kind of lost or missing her parents, maybe that's why she showed me the photo! I have no idea who this is, but I'm not freaked out yet. My husband is a little bit, though.

-Anonymous

The Little Ghost Girl Returns

Continuing from my previous story about the little girl ghost that would visit my house, I hadn't seen her for a very long time, probably not since the end of last summer. Well, yesterday morning, I was in my bed playing with my two children, now aged five and almost three, when my youngest daughter said, "Mummy, there is a little girl standing at the top of the stairs." I said, "Oh, OK, say hello and ask her her name. She waved to her and said, "Hello," and I asked what the girl said, and she told me that she didn't say anything but showed me the actions that the little girl had put her chin into her chest. She said she was sad. We carried on playing, but the children wouldn't go downstairs until the girl went away, which was about an hour later. My daughter said she was just standing watching us. My daughter also said that the little girl was wearing a pink dress and had white/yellow hair. We opened my daughter's blinds in her bedroom and went downstairs, then we all went into the lounge. About two hours later I went upstairs and saw that my daughter's bedroom blinds were closed, my daughter said the little girl did it because she was being naughty!

-Anonymous

The Stuff of Nightmares

I have had a few odd experiences happen to me. We went to look at a house and were left the key to go and look around one time. It was empty and had been renovated, ready for sale, and as we drove away from the property, I looked back and saw an outline of a figure in the spare room window. It really gave me the creeps.

We ended up buying the house back in 1993. One night after having a disagreement, I slept in the spare room where I had seen that figure. When asleep, I had this horrid feeling that someone was trying to strangle me. Weight was on my legs just like someone was sat on them. My sister-in-law had strange feelings in my dining room, as did my mum and dad, and also when they stayed over in the spare room to babysit.

We did up the spare room, and it became our son's room. My husband and I split up, and most nights, the boys would end up in my room because they said they were scared of the monster. We had new spotlights put in the house, and they used to dim on and off all by themselves. The spare room window was made of plastic and would steam over where I had seen the figure appear that day.

One night I was putting the boy's clothes away when the lights went off. The boys said, "What's that, mum?" so I just told them that I could twiddle my nose and dim the lights so as not to scare them. It would also go very cold in the house when there were signs of activity happening. The boys' toys would go off by themselves in the middle of the night. It was quite spooky.

A cousin was coming over to stay, so I moved the boys to one of the attic rooms, so the spare room was empty ready for their arrival. Later that day, one of my friend's came round with her husband to collect a buggy for her baby. Normally the baby would put her arms up for me to pick her up, but she cried in both the dining room and the spare room. It was very strange.

A friend of mine said that her husband was into talking to spirits, so one day, my friend, her husband, myself, and a work colleague went up to the room. He said that he felt the porthole where all of the activity came from was the window that the figure had been seen in. He then said for me to walk into my room opposite as whatever this was, would follow me from room to room as it was attached to me. He then put a marker down on the floor under one of the toys in the bedroom, which continuously used to go off by itself. He wanted to do a séance that night. I was a bit unsure at first, but I eventually gave in.

At 8 pm that night, my friend and her husband, my work colleague, and two other friends came round. My friend's husband went up to the bedroom where the marker had been left under the toy and noticed it had been moved. No one had entered that room since they had left earlier that afternoon. When he came back downstairs, we started the séance, and we all joined hands. He started to talk to the spirit. I had one of my other friends holding on to my right hand when he then collapsed onto the floor, swearing that he had been kicked in the back of his knee.

My friend's husband said to join hands again and told me what to say because he thought it would work better. I started to say what he told me when suddenly he went down into a heap on the floor. My friend and work colleague were in tears by then, so he held my left hand again, and the circle was shut down.

We all went into the kitchen, and two of my friends suddenly heard a child singing upstairs. About fifteen minutes later, my friend's husband went back upstairs as he wanted to take some still shots with his camera to see if he could catch anything paranormal. I was kneeling on the wooden floor when my lap went icy cold. He asked me if I felt anything unusual, and I told him that my knees had gone icy cold.

We then joined the others back in the dining room and looked at the shots that he had just taken when we noticed lots of orbs in the pictures all around me. The one of me sitting on the floor had a blue figure of a small child perched on my lap with its arms wrapped around me. I then filled up

41

with tears as it was upsetting that it was a small child. We just couldn't believe what we had captured on camera.

Not long after, I had a friend round for tea one night who did not believe in spirits at all. However, his face said something different. He said that the child spirit had run past him at the dining table whilst he was sat there, then another night we were doing the dishes in the kitchen, and he swore that the child was standing beside him. Sometimes when I am in the lounge, it's like a child can be heard running across the floorboards in my bedroom. I have had other experiences in my room where it felt like something was pinning my legs down and again a feeling like arms were around my neck. Around this time, one of my work colleagues would not go upstairs to the toilet because they were just too scared. So many strange things have happened in that house!

-Julie

Haunted Dreams

I still live in this house, but everywhere I live, I can sense things, but it's only in this house that things have happened. I've had this house blessed twice since I've been living here (twelve years). My youngest son was one year old when we moved here, and he started to get night terrors very severely. He would scream like someone was attacking him. I'd go into his room and talk to him very softly so that he would calm down. It always happened from 10:00 pm until 4:00 am every night until about two years ago. When I first had this house blessed, the lady went straight to my son's room and told me there's a little girl here who can't find her mummy, so she goes through to my son in his sleep to get my attention because I'm a mum. There is also a male presence that I can feel here too. I always hear heavy footsteps coming up the last few stairs when I'm in the bath. It's really like someone is there, so I call out, but no one is there. We all see dark shadows out of the corner of our eyes in this house. It is very strange.

-Marie

Chapter 5 - The Unexplained

The Mysterious Shopping Trolly

I was with my cousin Dave. We were driving down the road towards L'Aumone (Castel) at about 3 am. As we drove around the corner, we saw a shopping trolly spinning round and round in circles at a great speed in the middle of the road. It then crashed against the pavement. We could clearly see that nobody was there to cause this to happen, and there was absolutely no way that a strong wind was spinning the trolly. There were no driveways nearby where anyone could have been standing or run off down it. It was so weird.

-Robert

Heaven Scent

I was reading a book about two in the morning when I suddenly smelt a really sweet perfume. It definitely wasn't mine as I only had one, which was vanilla scented. I just couldn't figure out where it was coming from. It just kept coming and going this sweet-smelling perfume scent. It was very strange.

A couple of days later, I mentioned this to my mum, who told me that she has been having exactly the same thing happen in her house.

-Ellie

The Mysterious Knocking

I heard a loud knocking on my bedroom door once when I knew that I was alone at home. I was really scared, too scared to come out of my room or to approach the door, but I did after a few minutes and saw that the front door was still locked, with no one else in the house. It only happened once, but I was strangely aware that it was something abnormal. Even the knock was kind of hollow sounding.

-Kim

A Tap on the Shoulder

I'm living down Forest Lane (St Peter Port), and a while back, whilst I was in bed, there were a few nights where I felt as if someone was tapping me on my right shoulder. I shrugged it off and kept it low-key, thinking it was possibly muscle cramps or something else.

I'm not a huge believer in all this, but oddly enough, my girlfriend slept over a couple of weeks after my incident; she freaked out and hid under the covers, clinging to me. I asked her what was wrong, and she said, "Someone was tapping me on the shoulder." OK, I thought, this is interesting.

Ever since then, we really can't shake off the feeling that we are not alone in the house. It's a very strange feeling.

-Carl

The Ring Box

One night when I was at home, I experienced something very strange. I had a box with some rings in it that my dad had given to my mum when he was alive, which were on my cabinet when suddenly the ring box went flying off it when I wasn't looking, but I heard it clatter to the floor! I didn't hear anything slide that could have knocked it off the cabinet. The strange thing was this happened on the day that it would have been my dad's birthday.

-Ellie

Who Slammed the Door

One night after I had moved into my new house, I got up and went to the bathroom. My kid was sleeping in my bed at the time as we only had one set up. As soon as I went to leave the bathroom to go back to bed, the bathroom door slammed shut. I froze for a couple of minutes as I couldn't believe what had just happened. I opened the bathroom door and realised that the bedroom door was also shut. My kid was fast asleep snoring, so it wasn't him. There were no windows open either.

This doesn't happen when I'm on the phone or when my kid is awake. It only happens when I'm awake and when I'm not on the phone talking to somebody. It also happens when I'm in a different room than my kid when he is sleeping.

46

-Anonymous

The Glowing Green Torso

I had moved to St Martin's the Saumarez Mill area, and on my way home one Saturday night around 12.20 am at the end of the road after the turning into the estate, I saw (and this is going to sound crazy) what looked like a green glowing half a torso walking across the road. It was literally just the legs. I had been drinking that night, but I was nowhere near drunk.

-Kylie

The Broken Vase

I lived at the top of cornet Street (St Peter Port) by the cornerstone pub. One day I was rushing out of the flat to get to work, and as I ran down the stairs, I knocked a vase with roses in it over, and it smashed and shattered all over the window ledge and stairs. I was late for work, so I just left it and locked the door behind me. I got home from work ready to clear up the mess, but the vase was back on the windowsill, intact with all of the roses inside of it. I was sharing the flat with my brother at the time, but he was away travelling in Australia. No one else had been in there, spooky!

-Beccy

The Attention Seeking Ghost

I was alone downstairs walking in the kitchen in my father's home in Forest Lane (St Peter Port) when something threw a hair clip at me, and it landed in front of my feet. I saw it come past and land in front of me. It didn't spook me. I just thought it was rather odd!

-Carl

Spirit Visitors

I have had some strange things happen to me. My grandparents lived in Collings Road (St Peter Port). They had moved there in 1988. It was about 1999, and I was living with them. One night, I couldn't get to sleep, so I was lying there looking at the window when suddenly the next thing I knew, it felt like someone was alongside the bed behind me. The quilt cover lifted by itself and moved towards the bottom of my bed to expose me. I quickly turned over, but no one was there. I was freaked out.

In the place that I live now, I see lots of orbs floating about. When I first moved into the house two years ago, I was sitting on the sofa when something started moving the cushion part of the sofa, it freaked me out a little bit, but luckily nothing has happened since.

-Jon Vokes

Unexplained Physical Touch

Some friends and I used to meet at my flat in La rue de Rocquettes in St Andrews by Talbot Valley. Some nights after a few drinks, we would walk to Fauxquets Valley to see if we would see anything ghostly. This one night, we were walking down the lane just up from Fauxquets House, and I needed to have a pee, so the others carried on walking, and I made sure that no one was around and dropped my trousers. Then the next thing I knew was that there was someone's hand on my bum. I quickly turned around, trying not to fall over my trousers, but there wasn't anybody there. I called out to the others, but they didn't believe me because I had been drinking.

-Jon Vokes

Seeing Is Believing

My haunting started when I was around 11 years old and lived with my dad, sister, and one of my brothers in a house at Le Picquerel estate (Vale). Our house was directly opposite some bunkers next to the beach, and as kids, we were able to get into the bigger bunker covered with brambles. The big bunker had big rooms inside, so some of the older kids on the estate used to go in and drink and smoke there. We heard a story that a shoebox was found inside the big room that contained some small bones, possibly a child's. Whether that bit was true or not, I don't know, but at night time, you could hear a baby cry, and sometimes, you would see a figure of a man walking towards the bunker that could be seen from our back garden.

My dad put a swing for us siblings in our back garden, where we would scrape our feet on the ground. Slowly, this hole started to show. It ended up being on the steps that led down to the bunkers, which meant the house was built on top of tunnels leading to the bunkers. So, after this occurrence, my dad covered it over with more ground.

I remember one night during summertime, we were sent to bed whilst my dad was popping over next door for a coffee. My sister was always the first to fall asleep; she slept as soon as her head hit the pillow. I was in the top bunk, and I could hear her snoring. I just lay there, planning what I was going to do the next day. My bedroom door was closed, and my brother was in his own bedroom when suddenly, I felt this vibration in the wall behind my bed. Then I felt a spirit come through the wall and go through me. My body was stiff and ice cold; I didn't know what to do. It frightened the life out of me, and I jumped over the side of the bunk bed, making a run downstairs and grabbing the phone next door. I told my dad what had happened; he tried to call me down by saying, "Don't worry. Concorde had flown over. Go back to bed, close your door, and I will be there in a minute." I did as I was told, and sure enough, I heard him come in the door and walk upstairs. Nevertheless, it seemed like a while before he opened my door to make sure I was OK. Dad did come in and told me I was safe as he was home now. He said he would be locking the house up and going to bed then. I couldn't sleep till I knew he was in bed.

It wasn't until several years later when I was grown up, that my dad admitted that when he tried to come into my room that night, something stopped him from opening the door. I know that a few years before that incident when my mom was still living with us, she woke up a few times to see a monk kneeling down at the side of her bed. I was always told that monks were a sign of protection, as when my dad was a fisherman, he spotted monks standing on rocks in the middle of nowhere.

When I was 13 or 14 years old, I moved in with my mom and my youngest brother into a house at Le Genet Estate, Castel. Silly things would go on there, too - the lights flashed on and off in the house, and we could hear someone getting out of Mum's bed and walk across the bedroom floor while we watched TV in the lounge. The footsteps were very clear, and you could hear them easily. Then, one night, we heard a loud bang come from the landing. We rushed to see what it was and saw a piece of plaster in perfect shape lying on top of the stairs. We looked up and noticed that it was from the ceiling, but it honestly looked like someone had taken the end of a broom and pushed it hard into the ceiling. We found it very strange, so my brother went up into the attic to see it may be a roof tile or something had caused this, but there was no explanation for it.

Fast forward two when I was 22 years old, I had two children with my husband. We moved into a flat in Mount Durand, St. Peter Port. It was very cold inside the house as it was all white with stonework. There, my kettle would often boil on its own. And I clearly remember this one evening when I had put my daughters to bed while my husband was working late. I was on the telephone talking to my mum, facing a picture on the wall. I had my eyes on that picture when it started spinning around. I was freaking out on the phone; it spun so fast that it flew up the wall and smashed itself. I was petrified.

We then bought our first home in Victoria Road, St. Peter Port. It was a converted house turned into two flats we had upstairs. By this time, I had three children, so my two daughters and son shared a bedroom that would have been the attic. My daughter told me about a little boy who played in the bedroom with them and his mummy, who came out of the cupboard under the eaves and told them stories. I put it down to their imagination until one night, I was decorating our lounge and closed the door to paint. That is when I heard knocks on the door, but every time I opened it, no one was there. This happened four or five times, then the next time I opened it, I saw that there was a little boy sitting on the stairs dressed in rags. He looked like a chimney sweep boy and disappeared just like that. I never saw anything in that flat after that.

Later on, I moved to a statehouse at Rue de Grons, St. Martin). I never had anything strange happen there, but then did a house swap to Rue Perruque in Castel. The house made for the back of King Edward hospital, and strange things went on there - the stop would go missing, etc. By this time, I had five children in my bedroom, where there was a hatch to the attic; it had a built-in wardrobe. No matter what, if that wardrobe door was opened even just a bit, I could not sleep. I knew something was in there watching me. I felt it many times and would even be pushed out of my bed. In my son's bedroom, there was an airing cupboard, and you could hear scratching sounds coming from in there. Besides, things like stuff getting misplaced then found in random places kept going on.

One day, the kids had all gone to school. I unlocked the back and front doors and went up to rest for an hour. I fell asleep, and just then, I felt a really hard kick in my back. I fell on the floor and ran downstairs, unlocking the front door. I ran to my friend who lived across the road. She thought that someone was inside the house, so she came back with me to check it out. What we hadn't bargained for was we were locked out of the house while the key was on the inside of the door. Whatever it was had turned that key to lock us out. My friend managed to climb through the window to open the door, but no one was around.

Roughly seven years ago, I moved into Le Guelle flats in St. Peter Port with my youngest daughter. Sometimes when things were bad, I would have dreams of an Indian chief. He would always appear in my dreams until one day when I thought I was going to die and saw him standing in my bedroom doorway. There was no expression on his face; he just looked very serious but never spoke. He just stood there, and I could see every line on his face. I saw the coloured feathers in his hair. I couldn't shake off this image of the Indian, so I thought I was going to have to speak to someone who would actually believe what I was seeing. I spoke to my nan, and it turned out that my great great grandfather was a West Indian. She told me that they were all about protection, so I now know that I was going through hell, thinking I was going to die while being protected by him.

The next house that I lived in, my daughter and I did not like at all. We felt the eeriness of it as soon as we walked in there and would hear banging on the stairs throughout the day and night. My daughter would not sleep in our own bedroom there, and she wouldn't go to the bathroom on her own either. She was so scared she slept in my bed. We would also hear scratching on my bedroom wall. We had the box room in the house, too, so my sister stayed over sometimes and lived in that room as there was enough room for a single bed and bedside unit. She would put her cigarette packet and phone on the unit and literally watch her cigarette packet sliding across the unit all by itself.

While living there, a very close family member passed away. I went to see him at the chapel of rest and gave him a kiss, but I didn't like how cold he was. I had a memory bear made from his clothes and would keep him on the dressing table next to my bed. However, I had this really bad habit of wrapping this bear up in a blanket as I didn't want him to be cold like the person was when I kissed him goodbye. Every night, I made sure that he was wrapped up properly and said goodnight to him. This went on for a long time until one of my daughters came to stay the night. She was in the box room, but as soon as I walked into my bedroom, I sensed something wasn't right. I walked to the dressing table to do my usual routine of wrapping the bear up, but something stopped me. I turned around and on the other side of my bed were these bright, beautiful colours swirling around. I watched in amazement, but I wasn't scared; I actually felt very calm. They soon disappeared, though, and as I went to wrap the bear in the blanket, I realized it was gone. It has now been six years, and I haven't wrapped the bear up since that day. I'm pretty sure what I saw that night was my family member letting me know that they were OK and not cold anymore; it really did bring peace.

Unfortunately, my health started deteriorating, and I had to move into a disabled home with my youngest daughter and my now husband. We have been here four years now, and my husband has always been a non-believer. These strange occurrences have been with me always and are still here. My husband has started seeing shadows in my lounge, and I, too, hear noises of things being moved in my kitchen. My husband wasn't having any of it, and one night, my daughter sat in the bathroom to cool down and call it in her book. We were in the lounge when we heard a loud crash. My daughter screamed, so we went to look and see what had happened. I had some tiny little ornaments on top of the mirror light that had been there since I've moved in with my daughter. My daughter said that it went really cold although the window wasn't open, and one of these ornaments dropped and smashed into the sink.

My husband still wasn't believing that it was anything paranormal, so in anger, I said to him, "You wait until something happens to you, and then you will believe it." Sure enough, the next day, he was in the shower, and I was outside in the garden. I could hear him swearing, so I came inside and asked him what was wrong. He said that the water was running fine one minute, and the next, there was nothing. The actual shower head had turned itself into the wall all by itself. We tried all sorts to explain and debunk what had happened, but there wasn't anything that could explain why the shower head did that. Also, my husband started to experience things like his long hair would get touched; it felt like his hair was being stroked and yanked at times - not hard but enough for him to notice. He would feel sharp pricks in his arms and legs, which I have also experienced, and it still happens today.

Then he started noticing the shadow man in the lounge and the flashes of light in the house. He now tells me that he definitely believes in this kind of thing on the activity picks up around certain times of the year. We also hear disembodied voices, like a woman's voice that says "hello," in my bedroom. We also hear a man talking, but sometimes, we can't work out what he is saying, and sometimes it's like there's a conversation going on. We see mists form on the lounge floor, and we also see a black cap-shaped shadow shoot across the ceiling in the lounge. We see orbs all of the time throughout the house.

All the strange things have happened during the summertime. We used to keep the bedroom window open, and in the early hours, we would hear something whistling in the garden. I had to make sure the window was closed. Now, too, things go missing then reappear, and the curtains in the lounge would move. We all have our favourite places to sit on the sofa; my daughter sits on the two-seater, while my husband and I sit on the three-seater on each end. If we go to hold hands or he puts his hands on my legs, it literally goes ice cold in between us, so I don't think that whatever is in the house likes holding hands.

We know when it is around as you feel the static and the cold bursts of air in the property. I always ask politely to move away, and it does, so we have just adjusted to living here for four years now. It obviously doesn't mean any harm, or else it would have done something by now. It doesn't frighten any of us. It is just that sometimes when it's the early hours of the morning and everyone else is asleep while I am up, I do get an uneasy feeling. Nevertheless, I know I'm not in any danger.

Anonymous

Tick Tock Terror

We stayed in a self-catering flat on Route Militare, St. Sampson, that was haunted. We heard the sound of an old grandfather clock ticking loudly that would follow you around the house day and night. We called it the walking clock. My dad noticed a deep ticking sound first in his room - like a grandfather clock - but he never told anyone at the time. I was about ten years old when I was woken up by the clock ticking sound that seemed to be walking around. My sister and I slept in the kitchen area when it walked around us, and after a while, it walked out of the door near the bottom of my bed. It happened more than once a while on holiday, and I remember hiding under the duvet and sweating a lot. This one year, when we stayed upstairs, my auntie was in the flat when she felt the ticking come upstairs, and she hid in the bathroom, scared.

Anita

What's Going On?

One night, my housemate, who doesn't believe in ghosts, and I sat at the kitchen table, drinking wine and chatting. He sat opposite me, and there was a mug to his left on the table, almost in the middle of the table. The mug had been left there from earlier in the day and had a teaspoon in it. We were chatting away when the teaspoon suddenly jumped and rattled against half of the mug. My housemate looked at me and said, "Did you see that?"

"Yes, I did," I replied. I thought that he was winding me up and had kicked the table. He swore he wasn't winding me up that night.

Laura

Ghost Frequency

I bought an old World War II German radio set. I was upstairs the previous night at 2 a.m. and heard a noise downstairs in my radio shack, where the said radio was. As soon as I entered the shack, it stopped. It was not even plugged in. My cat hisses and runs away from the radio whenever she is near it. Usually, she sleeps near my stuff.

Dieter

Extreme Fear

I've always found Fort George and that area scary. My dad was walking down Coulbourne Road, St. Peter Port, one night and had come home scared to death because he had seen an 'old shaggy dog.' He said it didn't quite look like a dog and that it was strange-natured. He had a few drinks that night, but he was terrified; he had run all the way home because he said that it had made him feel uneasy. I doubt it was a sheep as he said that it was tall and very skinny. My dad doesn't believe in the paranormal, but I'm sure that night he did. He was so scared, and I've never seen him like that. He also said that the creature looked old and was really big and skinny, running around. It then stopped in front of him and stared, and this was when he ran.

Anonymous

Most Haunted

My 1870's Victorian property is either haunted or has residual energy reoccurring. This all started in 2008 when I moved into the property. On one occasion, my partner and a guest all saw and heard a glass move in my lounge glass cabinet by itself. A chair was overnight placed on the base of a staircase nowhere near to where it belonged, and it was also a little eerier than it usually was. Overnight again, a bowl of fresh red roses in my lounge had been taken out and placed into groups of four, circulated to correspond with our sitting positions. I am definitely aware of one major cold spot within the lounge area that could have significance.

I just live with it all as the house has no ill feelings or bad intentions. I am just living with another person or energy that I can't see who comes and dwells within the house. I also think that the presence definitely knows that my partner and I are aware of them being there, but they do not infringe.

Update a couple of weeks after this happened:

Just before leaving the house last weekend for a weekend trip, I was packing up some essentials when I felt and heard a massive 'boom' from above me. It was above my lampshade in the lounge, and the ceiling lampshade shook. The contents on my table dropped off, and I thought that there had been a structural collapse upstairs in the bedroom. I then went upstairs to check, and nothing had been moved. The noise was definitely located from underneath my bed upstairs – the cause definitely unknown. I was quite shaken up, though.

Marie.

Scared to Death

I remember around 25 years ago at Le Foulon, St. Peter Port, some friends and I were doing the usual who's brave enough to walk through a graveyard at night stunt. No matter how hard we tried, we could not walk through to the old part from the new. It was around 1 o'clock in the morning when it seemed as if there was an invisible barrier blocking our way; we had a very strong sense of foreboding, and the hairs stood up on the backs of our necks. I had never felt so scared before. It was an unreal experience.

Another time I tripped over a gravestone, and when I looked at the date on it, it said my birthdate. That was a scary experience, I can tell ya!

Tanja

The Old Cottage

This is not the first time things like this have happened to me when I was little. At about six years old, I lived in an old cottage near the quarry in Vale, and one day when I was in my bedroom, I heard a really loud snore. I remember freaking out big time, and my gran came into my room to get me. I remember her saying, "You only said that so that you can stay up and watch Benny Hill." I'll never forget that snore for as long as I live. I lived in that house when I was a newborn, and I shared that room with my mum. She told me that I would stand in my cot and point to the corner of the room, but there would be nothing there.

Rachel

Unexplained Events

I hear a lot of footsteps day and night in the house that I live in. Strange things have always happened, like the shower turning itself on in the middle of the night. Things have been knocked off the top of the fridge, and even the Siri on my phone has gone off bang on midnight on April fools. Whatever it is, it has never hurt us, and we have never seen it either. Sometimes you can sense it in the house; other times, the house feels calm and quiet.

Marie

Red Streams

I used to live on the Les Genats Estate, Castel. There was something strange there; I saw it on many occasions, but to this day, I cannot figure out what it was; it had two almost LED-like eyes that left streams behind as they travelled. One night, I was stuck in my bed due to some incredible force that felt like I was being sat on and pushed down by something. Another time, in broad daylight, my stepdad and I saw the streams jumping up and down in my brother's room. I lived in the house between the ages of three and ten years old, so I left around 1996. There were a number of incidents and just a general funny feeling on that whole estate, especially the top and bottom part, and very much so by the bridge. I wasn't really overly scared, but the curiosity about the red streams has always stayed with me. I have lived in haunted flats and houses and have encountered ghosts, but I've never seen or heard of anything like that one at the Les Genats. Something tells me if I saw it now, I wouldn't be so blasé.

Anonymous

The Chimney Sweep

My son used to be obsessed with the Priaulx Library in St. Peter Port. Every time we passed it in the car or walked by, he would tell me all about when he was a little boy. He said he used to go up the chimneys to clean them and coughed so much that his chest really hurt. He would get very emotional whilst telling me this story. It was really strange as he started talking about this from about the age of two years old, and it carried on until he was six or seven years old.

Sami

The Hellhound

My brother and I saw a huge black dog one night in the lanes by the plant centre; it was jet black with red eyes and was built like a bear. It scared us stiff, but it took a defensive stance. So, I told my brother to walk with his bike by his side and to keep next to me so that if an attack occurred, I would be the first to take the hit. It never lunged or anything. It just stood its ground growing, and it disappeared when we got halfway down the lane. We kept our eyes on it the whole time when suddenly it just vanished. I know it wasn't a real dog because this was the thing of nightmares.

Carl

A Warning from Above

My husband had an experience when he was younger; he was out bike riding with his brother and suddenly heard a voice say ''stop.'' He stopped and asked his brother what was wrong. His brother replied that he hadn't said anything. It turned out that there was an open manhole in the road, and if he hadn't stopped, he would have gone down it. He believes it was his dead brother who had warned him.

Angela

A Ghostly Presence

A few years ago, my husband and I lived in a wing attached to a large house on Oberland's road in St. Peter Port. We decided to move houses, and once we had moved most of our belongings out, one dark evening, me and my daughter went back there to get the last few things. I had my arms full of items when my daughter, who was seven years old at the time, pushed past me through the door as I was turning off the light for the last time, ready to leave. My daughter shouted out, ''Hold on! Wait for me first,'' which shocked me as I had felt what I described - a child rushing past me only seconds before. I quickly locked the door, and we were gone!

Nicola

The Missing Toy

My daughter's favourite bed toy went missing, and she was distraught for a night. My hubby and I searched everywhere for it but found nothing. The next morning, I asked out loud for it back. I turned around, and it was in the baby bath right behind me. Both of us had checked there the night before.

Anonymous

The Ghost on the Stairs

One story that my sister-in-law told me was that she had visited a friend's house once and went in to use the toilet. To get to it, you had to go upstairs; she said she was walking up the stairs and felt someone brush past her, and without thinking, she said, "Sorry." Then she realized there wasn't anyone there. She turned around and went back outside to tell her friend, and they said, "Oh, you've met our ghost then." Needless to say, she didn't go back in for the loo.

Angela

The Disappearing Scarecrow

This experience happened in 1983-1984 when I had my pony. I often hacked through the valley, and one day, I was riding down from the Fauxquet side towards the Kings Mills. There were two large meadows on the right side, and I noticed what I thought was a scarecrow in the top part of the first meadow as I passed. It was about this time that I was diagnosed with short-sightedness and told I needed glasses for distance, so I squinted at this figure, trying to work out if it had a head or not. After a while, I lost interest. However, I will say this was one of the uncomfortable days riding through the valley because when I glanced back towards the scarecrow, it wasn't there. What's more, I saw it further down in the text field. After much more squinting and trying to rationalize that it was a scruffy farmer and thinking I'd missed the farmer moving the scarecrow I saw. I thought once I got to the bottom of the lane and around the corner, I would be able to get a better view. I never took my eyes off it from then until I reached the corner where the hedge obscured my view; when the field came back into sight - maybe after a few minutes or so - there was no sign of the scarecrow or anything else.

Anonymous

The Headless Scarecrow

In the early '90s, I was riding my motorbike through Rue des Fauxquets to my girlfriend's house, and as I turned into the valley from Candie Road, I noticed that the field on the right had been harvested for whatever had been growing in it and all that was left were the stumps of the plants and a headless scarecrow towards the far side of the field. I thought it really weird to have a scarecrow without a head in a field of nothing. I must have ridden on about 50 meters or so and looked back to see if what I saw was correct. I turned around to see the scarecrow was now next to the wall of the road where I had just ridden past. Needless to say, I didn't hang around.

Andy

The Beautiful Garden

When I was a child, I lived in St. Sampson's, and my brother and I used to play in the fields opposite our house. Adjoining these fields was an old house with walled-off gardens. One day, we ventured further and looked through the tall gates to see the garden; we were amazed at how beautiful it was with lots of topiary and owls, etc. In there, it looked like a Victorian garden. We were so impressed with it we took our friends along the next day to show them. When we looked at them, it was completely different - just a normal modern garden, no topiary, nothing. It was so weird that we saw such a beautiful place the first time and the next, there was nothing. I'll never forget it; the house was spooky with all these latticed windows. Did we see a glimpse of the past, I wonder?

Angela

Message from Heaven.

Something strange happened one day. My hands-free phone had been playing up in my car and wouldn't answer my 'Phone when it rang'. Then suddenly, at 4:10 pm in the afternoon, it decided to work, and it was a call from my stepdad to say that my mum was there and he didn't know what to do. Now the thing is, my mum died in September 2019.

I told him that I would sort something out and call him back. I had just parked my car at work, and when I went in, they asked me if I was okay as I looked like I'd seen a ghost. I explained what had happened and said I didn't know what to do. It was a shock as my stepdad doesn't have dementia as far as I was aware. I phoned the doctor and arranged for the on-call doctor to go around to his house, and I also called my husband to go and see him.

When my husband got there, my stepdad searched the house for my mum, and my husband was worried that my stepdad would hurt himself when he was trying to go upstairs where he doesn't usually go as his balance wasn't very good. My husband went and looked upstairs for my mum, and when he came down, my stepdad had fallen, and he couldn't get him up. My husband then called me and explained what had happened, so I told him to call an ambulance.

To cut a long story short, it turned out that he had a urine infection and was quite poorly affected. That was the third time he had fallen in 3 weeks, and he had ended up in a hospital where they struggled to get his heart rate right and blood pressure under control.

Now that day, he could have been hallucinating due to the infection, but I like to think that maybe my mum visited him so that he would phone me, and we would get him the help that he needed as he lives on his own. He was convinced she had been there, and when I was allowed to see him in A&E hospital, the first thing he asked me was whether we had found my mum and if she was okay.

Nicky.

Signs from the Afterlife

I lived at La Vrangue, (St Peter Port) for roughly five years with my mum and brothers. Then, a few years later, I took over the house with my children for another five years. We had some strange things happen in that house; we used to have stuff thrown down the stairs, things would go missing, and we would hear noises upstairs when no one was there. I only really felt comfortable when I was in my bedroom.

Anonymous.

Ghoulish Goings-on.

My strange experience was when I was 12 years old in 1984 around Sandy Lane to the L'Islet dolmen area (St Sampson). I remember walking around there, I used to take photographs, and it was wintertime. I remember turning around and feeling like someone was following me several times that day. I have also felt a similar vibe at the reservoir too. I heard sticks crunching like someone was walking behind me, but no one was there.

Greg.

A Grave Discovery.

When he was about five years old, my little brother was walking through a cemetery with the family and asked why a man standing far away was all wet. My parents took him over to see where and saw that the gravestone said, 'lost at sea!'

Kyle.

Strange Sightings.

I used to live in a house that was haunted. One day, I was outside talking to my neighbours, and I could see my son dancing in his room. I went up to see him, and he was fast asleep – but we all saw him jumping and dancing around in his bedroom! I used to close the bedroom doors (in the same house), and they would open while we watched. It wasn't the wind blowing them open as the door was tight against the carpet and would have to be pushed open. Also, something or someone used to pull my bed covers down off me too!

Another time I remember walking down Candie Road, and an old boyfriend shouted out to me as he was driving down the road - I didn't know at the time that he had just committed suicide the night before. That was very spooky and hard to come to terms with. I know even to this day, it was him, though!

Tina.

The Dead of Night.

My sister-in-law once told me that when her husband got out of bed in the night, she felt the mattress sink like he was getting back in and when she reached out with her hand (she was still half asleep), something touched her hand, and when she looked, he wasn't there.

Another time, she actually saw the covers lift and quickly got out of bed to fetch her husband. As she was frightened, he told her it was the side of the bed his first wife had slept on (she sadly died). They got rid of the bed, and it hasn't happened since.

Angela

Chapter 6 - Orbs, Evps, And Unexplained Lights

The Red Orb

When I was about ten years old, I slept in my mums' bed a lot. I never liked my bedroom, but one night, I couldn't sleep, and something was telling me to turn over. I turned over, and my mum's alarm clock said it was 22.22 pm. I will never forget when I suddenly saw a big red floating orb swirling inside to the right-hand side of the alarm clock.

I turned around immediately and hid under the covers. I couldn't sleep for the rest of the night, and I was too scared to wake up my mum up or to even turn to face that way again. I was not dreaming. I have only ever seen it once. The atmosphere was so strange that night.

Also, in my old bedroom, the shelves used to literally fly out of the bedside cabinet, which would never break! I used to have crystals on the shelves. One crystal broke once, but the glass triangle shelves never broke, and the windows weren't open either. There was no draft, and no one was in there, nothing. You would come home to find them like that.

One-time, I heard it happen when I was outside in the back garden, so I ran in to see what had happened and found the shelves on the floor. My sisters and my brother also experienced it.

Sophie

The Strange EVP'S.

One of my last experiences was when I was snorkelling on Les Amarreurs beach (Vale), and I was using my GoPro. I didn't think anything of it until I watched the footage again, and I picked up several EVP'S of my name being called out. I think we counted around ten times that my name was said and some other words, but it was hard to make them out. Very crazy indeed.

Kylie

A Fright in the Valley

A couple of years ago, three friends and I were walking through Fauxquet Valley at night-time, and when we reached the far gate by the lane, we looked back down the track and saw a very quick flash of light. It was almost like a car's lights shoot straight across the track from one hedge to the other. But it was very strange as no cars were there. The light that we saw was quite big and bright, and it was at the far end of the track. We didn't have any torches with us as we thought that we were brave enough to be walking through without any source of light until we saw that strange light. Then we found it quite scary. The light was a quick flash, and we didn't hang around after seeing that. We legged it.

Sam.

The Derelict House.

One night when I was a teenager, a couple of friends and I went into a derelict house. It was in-between the chain house and Fauxquet Valley, it was closer to the chain house and on the right as if you were heading to the Kings Mills. The property had been derelict for a very long-time, and even though it was on the roadside, it couldn't be seen because of the overgrown hedging. When we were there at this house, we certainly felt spirit presences there. We suddenly got freaked out and decided to make a run for it back out to the car when all of a sudden, this big light came out of nowhere and chased us until we got near the Kings Mills. The strange thing was that this light was not the height of any vehicle. This was one very freaky experience that I've never forgotten.

Laura.

The Bright Circle of Light.

I used to live in Hauteville (St Peter Port), and I was convinced that my flat was haunted. We had many experiences there of taps turning on themselves, and the shower also used to turn on by itself with no explanation. My child was a newborn, and every time I used to put him down for a nap, I would lie down myself, and this clicking noise would start. I would open my eyes, and it would stop. Then I closed my eyes, and it began again and so on. I searched the room but could never find anything. It would never be heard when my eyes were open, which really did freak me out.

We had a small walled-in dark courtyard; I had a cigarette out there late at night. It was pitch black, and from the right-hand corner, this small but super bright circle of light slowly moved diagonally to the left, became brighter, then just disappeared! I told my partner about this, and he then said, ''I had seen the same thing but didn't want to tell you as I thought it might have scared you''. I'm guessing that it was an orb.

I used to feed my baby in the middle of the night in the lounge in silence and always felt a presence. There was just something not right; I used to always be looking over my shoulder. It was always a very cold flat, and the more I thought about it, the place never felt homely or comforting.

Jacinta.

Chapter 7 - The Spiritual Influence Of Grandparents

Lil.

Ellie used to sleepover at our place most weekends. When she was little, around three years old, I put her in the travel bed that we had. After listening to a story or two, I said "Night Night!" and she silently closed her eyes and went to sleep. I got up and sat in the corner of the room on the comfortable sofa.

After about ten-fifteen minutes, she called out, "Kimmie." I came back, and she said, "Nannie Kimmie, can you tell the lady to stop singing now?" "What lady, sweetheart?" I asked, and she pointed to the ceiling while saying, "That one up there". She was adamant that there was a ladies' face singing.

It happened another time in the same year. On that occasion, when I asked her who she was chatting with, she said it was a lady. I asked who she was, and she said, "Lil." That was my nan's name- who had passed away, and there was no way that she could have known that. I'm sceptical of things that I don't see myself, but this gave me goosebumps.

Kim.

The Visiting Granny.

We bought a bungalow in St Martin's thirty years ago, which was haunted by granny Gallienne apparently. Some nights, we used to think that we've heard her say something. Even the doors would creak as if they were being opened.

This happened for about a year, and then one night, when I was by myself in my bedroom, the door opened in a spooky manner without anyone trying to open it. I confronted the spirit upfront and spoke to her. I asked it why she couldn't rest. I told her that all was well and that I would look after her house and she must not worry anymore. To my surprise, that was it. It was the last time I had seen her. I never felt her around again.

Sandie.

Nan's Visit.

It was two days after my nan had passed away. I was in the bedroom with my mum who was upset at something and in tears when I saw a shadow go past the window. I quickly ran to the next room to see who it was. From where we were sitting, we could easily see a person go by. I just saw white hair, and it was my nan walking past. Suddenly, she just disappeared.

Anonymous.

Nan's Disapproval.

I was on my way to a spiritual church with my mum. We were in the car, and I lit a cigarette (mum hates me smoking). She wasn't happy and joked with me that nan was going to come through in church and tell me to quit. When we got to the spiritualist church, I was the first person selected to receive a message. To my surprise, it was my nan wagging her hand at me.

Anonymous.

Nan Knows Best.

I was 15 years old at the time, and my gran had passed away four years ago. One night, my family went to see a medium for reading, but I decided to go out to underage Club54 instead.

The next day my family told me that my gran had come through with a message saying that someone was missing (meaning me), and they mentioned that gran said to pull this up and that down. She had done the actions as if to pull a top-up and skirt down. That night, I was wearing a low-cut top and a short skirt.

Anonymous.

The Scent of a Ghost.

I have seen the spirit of my grandfather before, and I know that my nan is also with me quite a bit, along with other family members who are making their presence known. When my husband's mother died, she showed herself in the form of a red orb that swirled around his head, which then disappeared. My nan's spirit, when around, smelled like the kitchen that had just been cleaned with TCP. My granddad's spirit smells like tobacco, my husband's mums' spirit has a wood burner scent, and my husband's dad's spirit has an old man's smell.

Chapter 8 - Creepy Castles, Forts, German Bunkers, And Haunted Hospitals

The Ghost Hunt.

I was helping a ghost hunting group at a private property where they owned a part of the Mirus Battery. The group had been there a few times before, and we asked them not to give any information to my friend since it was essential for us to get validations.

We managed to get three German soldiers, two of which were drunk! They were a foreign worker who had been poorly treated and an old lady looking for her cat! They were all a bit confused about the lady, but she had been there before the place was built.

What was amazing was that one of the room's was flooded with rainwater while I was asking the spirit to come close and give us a sign. The water started to ripple across the room, and the more the group spoke to the spirit, the more it would ripple. It was going mad at one point, and you could see the shadows ripple up the wall's leaving the technical guys happy that night.

It was a great evening, and we validated what others before us had picked up! So many different ways that spirits can let us know that they are around.

Nikki.

The German Underground Hospital.

I can tune into spirit, and on one occasion at the German Underground Hospital, I picked up residual energy. There was a kitchen area where I picked up the energy of a chef! He was pacing and anguished at the fact that he only had an ample covering compared to others, and this was a real big deal for him! Maybe it had something to do with the islands not having enough supplies, and they were entering during the period of starvation!

Also, a poor soul at one of the tunnels that was never finished was badly injured. Rock's fell onto his back, and while he was in excruciating pain, he was then made to walk out of the tunnel, pushed to the ground, and never got back up! Several soul rescues have been done in there, so I wasn't sure if I'd pick up any activity these days.

Nikki.

The Transparent Couple.

My grandparents lived in the Vale and bought my family up there. My cousin and I decided to have a mooch one night, so we crept out of the house at Church Lane and went up to the Castle. It was definitely eerie, and our bravado ran out very quickly. We ran back down to the road and, for some reason, turned and looked back up the path and saw that there were a couple of people standing and looking at us, so we ran across to the other side of the road as we watched the couple come down to road level, but as we watched, a car came around the corner and to our horror, the headlight's shone straight through the couple standing there!

We were only twelve years old at the time, and as my cousin and I should not have been out and about at that time of the night. I swear, we ran so fast that we broke the land speed record getting back to Church Lane that night!

Jo.

The Strange Blue Light.

One day, I went to the German Underground Hospital with my friend, and when we were in the kitchen area, I saw a sharp blue light shoot across from the back towards the stove. My friend didn't see it, but when we were walking through the ward to leave, she stopped and told me to listen because she could hear a squeaky sound, like a wheel on a food or nursing cart being moved around.

Anonymous.

The Scary Man.

One afternoon, my partner and I went to Fort Grey and took the two-year-old that I looked after there. He was a really quiet, placid little boy who never kicked off and rarely cried, but he asked to be picked up, and he started screaming and shouting, "No, No, No" as soon as we walked in. I couldn't calm him down at all and had to go back outside.

We went back in, and he started crying and shouting again. We then went downstairs, and he was briefly alright, only to quickly turn to the stairs and shout, "No," again. In the end, we had to go out with him until he calmed down.

After a little walk around, we were able to take him back inside where he was still a bit nervous but much calmer than before. Before we crossed the road back to the pearl, we asked him if something was scary, and he straight away pointed at the Fort. I asked if it was a scary lady or a man. He said, "Man!"

Anonymous.

The Ghostly Male Voice.

I took a couple of Spanish students to the German Underground Hospital one year as they were staying with us for a week or so, we walked around until we got to one of the escape shafts and while we were there I heard a male voice near my ear saying something but not clearly. I looked at the Spanish kids and they were both staring at me with mouths open, I asked if they too heard the voice and they said "yes". We didn't see no one else in the tunnels while we were there. Weird!

Kylie.

That Spooky Feeling.

I know a lot of people have stories about the German Underground Hospital, but my only experience with spooky or ghostly occurrence was there at the hospital. It was about mid-afternoon, and my friend and I were walking her dog around the lanes near the underground hospital. We were both quite into horror things and haunted places, so we decided to peak our nose a little around the area. As we were about to enter, her dog kept whining and would flat out refuse to go in. We just looked around the entrance and a little on the inside, leaving the dog by the door as she would not come in. In about two minutes, it got really cold, and we decided that we should leave- it was spooky enough already, and as I touched a doorway inside of the hospital, her dog went crazy, and we just ran out of there. It was like we were in danger because my friend had never seen her dog act so crazy like that before. I haven't gone back, but I definitely wouldn't wander about in there on my own!

Anonymous.

One Scary Experience.

One day, I went to the German underground hospital and had a very scary experience in the morgue area where I saw a figure manifest in front of me, but I only managed to catch the back end of it on film. I also saw blue, glowing orbs with my own eyes, and I managed to catch a few on camera as well.

Kylie.

The Mystery Man.

Years ago, I went to visit a fortress on the island. It was winter when we went, so it was a rather gloomy day. I had my little sister with me at the time, and as we entered the building, we heard a noise and noticed that a man had appeared from nowhere. I don't know what he was wearing, but it was not from the 80s (when we went). He stood there for what seemed like ages and just disappeared. We both couldn't believe what we had seen.

Alison.

The Mirus Battery.

My night at the Mirus Battery was truly a horrible experience that is not easy to forget. The past is trapped there. You can feel it as soon as you enter. This is how I would describe it- I entered this bunker system in the mid 80's with a couple of friends. Our visit was from around 11pm to just before 2am. It was a warm July night. We entered the Mirus bunker, walked around its many rooms and corridors, remarking how well preserved it was! I remember I said that I bet if the cables were connected, the lights would still work! We sat on the floor in many rooms, talking and listening. We experienced strange sounds, smells, and sightings within this bunker system. There were whiffs of tobacco smoke. We could just hear snatches of German radio stations and distant voices.

At one point, we could hear footsteps in a room at a closer distance to us. On investigation, there was nothing that could have caused that. We certainly felt we were not alone that night. There was a presence with us, but it wasn't an evil one! It was one looking for something or someone. But at no point did we feel scared or threatened by this place.

Later on, we saw a shadow move slowly from one room to another. The area was noticeably colder for some reason. I was not alarmed by this as I have experienced this same cold spot feeling at St Martin's country hotel to a more dramatic degree.

As we left the Mirus Battery, we looked at the sloping walkway light up by moonlight to see what we could only describe as a German soldier standing as if to see us off! You could see his face and every part of his body seemed to be solid. At that point, we heard something moving in the nearby bushes.

When we looked again, he was gone.

I will never forget that night there. A number of people I have spoken to have seen ghosts (echoes of the past) of

German soldier(s) there or in the near vicinity of the Mirus Battery.

This place is certainly somewhere I'd like to investigate further. I was completely blown away by the idea of being haunted. I always said a big, "Yes" to it and, as I said earlier, the past is alive and well.

Dieter.

Monkey Man.

When my granddaughter was six years old, we took her to castle cornet. We were heading to the top where there was a telescope. When we were going up the steps to see the Condor come in, I said to her, 'I will race you to the telescope.' We were running towards it when she just stopped and started to cry. "What's up" we said, "Did you see that man? He looked like a monkey with long arms on the step. He was so ugly" the tears just poured down her face, and she was shaking.

It took us a good 10 minutes to get her down the steps again. I had to carry her down them. Afterwards, I told someone who gave tours around the Castle what my granddaughter had said, and they told us we'd heard a few stories about this before.

Roslyn.

The Screaming Man.

I heard a man screaming in either Russian or Polish right next to my ear. I was on one of the ghost tours at the Mirus Battery at the time. I looked around to see if anyone else reacted or heard it, but everyone just carried on walking down to a meeting room further inside. I felt sick and literally turned proverbial grey! I didn't say anything to anyone around me because I felt like an idiot. I thought that no one would believe me. I have, however, spoken to people about it since and have learned that Russian and Polish slaves were used to build the bunker, and many of them starved and died there. I had no idea what kind of slave labour was used for that building at the time until the tour guide told us all in the meeting room after I'd heard the voice. It was very moving.

Ann.

Dead Scary.

One experience that my brother and his mates had was when they were mucking about in a German bunker whilst waiting for one of their friends who hadn't arrived yet. They heard a noise, so they all kept really quiet, and then noticed a gleam of light and heard marching sounds.

At this point, they still thought that it was their mate arriving. Next, a German soldier marched into the room. He went to the middle of the room then just disappeared! They all jumped up, looked at one another, then ran; they were all so scared that they never went back there again. My brother was not easily scared, and it usually took a lot to convince him about strange things like this happening. My brother also told me they couldn't see what had caused that source of light to appear in that bunker that day.

Jackie.

Ghostly Sensation at the German Underground Hospital.

I've had a few odd experiences in the German underground hospital. On my last visit there, I went with my partner and three children I looked after (one was asleep, one couldn't talk, and the four-year-old walked with us). I get a very dizzy feeling the whole time I'm in there. I often looked over my shoulder because I thought I could hear something, but as we got to the Mortuary (I didn't know it was the Mortuary yet as I looked in the opposite ward), I got a feeling as if something was around. I just felt uncomfortable, and at the same time, my partner said, "This is the Mortuary," and as I turned to look at him, I could see a shadow behind him that disappeared in a blink of an eye. However, it made me double-take, and the four-year-old said, "I don't like this bit." I agreed, and we carried on walking. I've previously seen a laser-type light shoot around the kitchen, and I've heard a trolley rattling and squeaking while visiting here before. Very strange.

Anonymous.

Hospital Horror.

So, here's my story of the German underground hospital. This experience happened moments before I was taking a picture on my phone. I felt a swipe sensation across the back of my head, strong enough to blow my hair. As I turned and looked for the source of the air, nothing was there. I dismissed this, of course. I then turned and went into the Mortuary when a white mist/cloud image came at me and went over my left shoulder, enough for me to wince and kind of strike out as I did. I pressed the button on my phone to take a picture, and when I looked back at it later on, I could hardly make out the white in the picture. To this day, I have not found out what it was, but I still think it was really strange.

Gary.

Lurking in the Shadows.

One afternoon, my mum and I went to the German underground hospital with a friend. It was really quiet in there, and we were the only people there along with the receptionist. As we were walking down the corridor that had an unfinished way in it (the one with the dummies), we saw them, and it freaked me out so much, I jumped at the height of almost one foot into the air. Once I calmed down, I saw something move in the cage that the dummies were in. I don't know what it was, but I could hear footsteps all of the time when we weren't moving. At first, I thought it might have been the receptionist guy, but then we realised that he was still in the reception area.

We then walked through one of the wards when suddenly my mum felt something brush her face. It wasn't her hair (it is really short), and it wasn't her friend's or mine, because we were in other parts of the room, taking photos. It was really creepy. Alongside, my mum's friend took a photo and managed to capture half a body in the picture. It looked like a boy wearing a t-shirt and jeans, but the image only caught the right side of the body. Nobody was in front of our friend when he took the photo, which is creepy. I took a few pictures, and in one of them, there is a strange pale grey circle that wasn't actually on the ceiling.

Anonymous.

The Angry Officers.

I've done a few investigations in German bunkers on the island, and I think that they or their energy is still there. Some spirits get annoyed that we are in their bunker, especially as we are not German, and they make their presence and annoyance felt in various ways. It seems that most of them that hang around are officers in charge who haven't quite got the idea that they are not in charge anymore. We had one occasion where a member of the team had someone breathe heavily in their ear as if trying to scare them (which it did). We have heard a definite cough before, and mediums have picked up German officers who really don't want us there.

Camille.

Past Sounds of World War II.

I had permission to go around the privately owned part of the Mirus Battery emplacement used by Battletec a few years ago to see what I could experience. I didn't have any ghost detecting equipment, though, but I tried to record some video on my camera in the back corridor. However, it kept stopping the recording after one second. I tried this many times, and the same thing kept happening. When I went back outside and in the curved corridor by the gun pit, it worked normally. I also went into the other emplacements and didn't get this problem. I also heard gunshot sounds firing at me from two separate places. Single pistol gun shots were coming from inside the back wall from almost two metres in front of me on the left side in one of the four crew rooms. After experiencing the first shot, my camera would not record more than one second of video, which was strange as it was fine again after I was outside and I walked away from the site. The whole time that I was inside, it felt like I was being followed.

Martin.

A Creepy Night at Castle Cornet.

I've done a couple of investigations at Castle Cornet once with a medium, and we had some interesting results. Two of the groups, including the medium, were in the prisoners' walk when they heard loud footsteps walking up towards them. Another member of the group and I were standing near the bottom of the Castle when we saw something cross the walkway further up. We couldn't say what it was as it was too quick. We had also found some interesting photos taken in there, and we had a really fascinating photo taken in the area which they now use as a store in the part of the Castle that's not open to the public. We also took a photo of a dark shadow standing outside a window, and when we tried to recreate it, we realised that it was impossible for someone to have been outside or for someone to cast a shadow from inside.

Camille

Chapter 9 - Female Apparitions

The Grey Lady

My earliest recollection of what could have been a ghostly encounter happened whilst playing in the playground at Haute Capelles infant school (St Sampson). I must have been around six years old at the time, and I recall one of the girls from my class becoming a little bit scared, saying 'the grey lady' was standing next to me and quickly running away.

Being so young at the time, I didn't really think too much about it. I remember this girl repeating this a few times on different days. Eventually, she just stopped talking about the grey lady.

Was this just the imagination of a child making up stories in the playground, or was there really the ghost of a grey lady following me around, or possibly that she was attached to that particular area or building?

It wasn't until many years later that I as an adult really thought about what happened back then. Having such a keen interest in all things paranormal and reading many different accounts all about the numerous worldwide sightings of grey lady ghosts did make me think back to when I was a child that maybe this was a real-life ghostly encounter. I guess that this is a ghostly mystery that I will never really understand, but somehow that memory has always stayed with me.

It is said that children are more susceptible to seeing ghosts than adults due to having a much greater sense of awareness. Therefore, being a child, you are more open minded and observant to these kinds of spiritual entities. The area of Capelles has a long and interesting history. The site where the current school is situated has been used many times before as various different schools over the years dating right back to 1784. The Les Capelles Methodist church is also located next to the school.

Kate

Disappearing Old Woman

I was in my car driving up Vicky Road (St Peter Port) with my friend Jason about 11 p.m. when we saw an old lady dressed in a black shawl hobbling up the road in front of us. Then, suddenly, she just disappeared. I turned to Jason and said, "Did you see that?" He replied, "Yeah, an old lady...she disappeared...you see that too?" There was no explanation for her to just disappear into thin air.

Robert

The Old Lady

We have always spoken about funny things happening in our house and thought that it might be Dennis's brother playing jokes as he was that type. Dennis has never believed in anything paranormal, but when I was very ill in hospital, and they were not sure that I was going to make it or not, one night he woke up and saw an old lady with white hair was standing over him looking at him. He said that he had a shock and got hold of the sheet and put it over his head.

Jane

The Singing Lady

I have had a few weird creepy things happen to me, but I have never seen a ghost as an adult. When I was really little, though, I used to sleep over at my nan Kim's house. She said that once I got up in the middle of the night and said to her, "Nannie, can you tell the lady on the ceiling to stop singing? I can't get to sleep."

Ellie

The Lovely Old Lady

This is a lovely story. I was at a dowsing/healing gathering being held at one of my members' houses. We were sat in the large conservatory adjoined to the farmhouse when my eyes were drawn up to one of the windows. There was this lovely old lady looking inquisitively down at us all. Her energy was nurturing and loving. I told the lady of the house, and she said that two of her lodgers had seen her too.

The next time I was there I saw the old lady again; she

was enjoying the energy. that night I also had a chat with the lodgers and picked up that one of the lodgers was creative and could draw. I suggested they must draw her so as the lady of the house could see what this lovely spirit occupying her house looked like. She did draw her, and it was the same description I gave in which I never told them; it was such a lovely validation.

Nikki

The Whispering Woman

I used to live with my dad in a big old house near the Amherst school in St Peter Port. I always used to hear footsteps breathing and door slamming at night but tried to ignore them as much as I could. One night I had a friend over, and we were talking about lots of different things. When the conversation went onto the topic of death, the lights flickered and went out, and the room got awfully cold.

Another time in the same house, I was alone and decided to move my room around because I was bored. I was facing the window, and as I turned my head, it felt like I was being forced to do so. That's when I heard a woman whisper in my ear. I didn't understand what she said, but it was definitely a woman, and she didn't sound English. I was so shaken up I never slept over in that house again. The paranormal activity seemed to revolve around my room as I didn't experience anything like that sleeping in the other rooms of the house.

Gem

The Lady on the Piano

My stepfather told me a great story about the former Beau Sejour's house (St Peter Port), and it is one he and subsequently I believe with the utmost sincerity given the participant involved. One of his aunts, a credible Victorian lady not taken to flights of imagination, was called upon to visit the house one day, whereupon the maid showed her into the drawing-room to await the arrival of Mrs Dobree. The aunt sat down and subsequently noticed a lady in the corner of the room sat at a piano. They nodded at each other, and a lady began to play the instrument. After some time, Mrs Dobree came into the room and apologised profusely for detaining her guest so long, whereupon the aunt replied that it was not a problem because she had been amply entertained by the lady on the piano. But looking over to the corner of the room, she then saw that there was no piano or lady to be seen. Additionally, my stepdad has said that many workmen at the time reported unexplained events during the conversion of the estate into the leisure centre.

Paul

Babysitter from Beyond

When the kids were younger, and we had just moved into the house we now live in, my husband checked on the kids before going to bed. I was in the kitchen, and as he checked on the last one, he heard a woman say, "They're fine." He then answered her thinking it was me, but realised he could still hear me in the kitchen. He came in with such a look on his face. I asked him if he thought I'd followed him and asked if the kids were OK. He said, "No, the woman's voice said 'they're fine' like she had already checked on them." I found that rather lovely!

Anonymous

A Grave Encounter

I was in the older part of the Vale church cemetery visiting my grandmothers grave when I saw a lady with a bunch of flowers walking down the path towards me. I walked towards the path expecting to meet her on the way, but she had disappeared. I stood for several minutes, scanning the graveyard to see where she had gone, but there was no exit where she was, and she wasn't at any other graves. My daughter was in the car at the end of the pathway and saw no one.

The strange thing is my aunt had visited the same grave a few months back and said she saw a lady come and stand nearby, and she said hello to her, but then she also disappeared. The lady that my aunt and I saw looked like a modern, well-dressed woman, which is why we didn't think there was anything strange about her being there in the first instance.

Angela

The Lady in White

One day at our church hall, a four-year-old came up to me and said that there was a lady in the other room who told her friend not to go there. She said she was white. When I went to look, she pointed to the stage and some equipment that was up there. As someone else had mentioned seeing a lady in white in the hall once before, I think that maybe the little girl saw her too, and she heard her speak to them. I think it could have been a teacher as this place used to be a church of England school in Victorian days.

Anonymous

Ghost Mum

When I was a little girl, I used to scream for my other mum at night-time, and I remember a lady dressed in old clothes coming into my bedroom to comfort me whilst stroking my hair. My mum would then come into the room, and I'd be like "No, my other mummy." No one else would see anyone there.

Also, when I was a child, I could hear footsteps in front of me but no one would be there. As I was only young, I just thought it was funny at the time. I used to have dreams about a certain house that I'd never been in, but I would know the exact layout of the house. It was weird, but I stopped experiencing things as I got older.

Laura

The Creepy Cottage

There is a cottage in the Castel that is said to be haunted by an old lady ghost. There was a young boy who used to live there who had an imaginary friend that he used to talk to. He would also go on to describe this old lady ghost in detail. I was only 11 years old at the time and didn't know anything about this story back then. One day, we passed this house around 6 p.m., and I remember seeing this old lady in one of the small panes of glass in one of the windows. Creepy!

Dani

Ghost Bride

My hubby lived in the Round Chimney house in St Sampson's from 1950 until 1975. His grandmother lived in it before him, he told me that there is a spirit of a half bride half widow that appears in that house the top of her is dressed in white like a wedding dress and the bottom half is dressed in black. He also mentioned that there were many other strange goings-on in there, like an old French lady that you could hear shuffle along the passageway to the gas meter. You would hear the money go in and drop into the box; then, you would hear her shuffle away again.

There was also an altar in the back bedroom that had a chalk crucifix in there that was given away when my father-in-law moved out. The house was very old with a huge garden that went all the way down to the greenhouses. One day, they found a huge stone at the bottom of the garden that took four people all day to dig around it. They tried to move it but could not, so, knowing it was late, they all left it there and went to bed. They got up early the next morning to try and move the stone again, but it was gone. The stone had disappeared, leaving just a huge hole. There was no sign of it at all, only of where it had been the previous day.

Anonymous

Chapter 10 - Male Apparitions

The Strange Man

My auntie and uncle lived in one of the houses on the Chemin du Mont estate (Castel), and we used to stay there a lot on New Year's Eve. As I was one of the youngest, I always went to bed the earliest along with my brother and I remember, I kid you not, a man used to open the door with a weird face just staring at us. As I got older, I just forgot about what I saw until my brother asked my aunt if that strange man still lived there. My heart sank, and I realised that it wasn't just me who saw him.

Nicola

The Ghost with the Lantern

I used to live in Pedvin Street (St Peter Port) back in the 80s with my large family. We had a few strange things happen, but nothing that really scared us. My sister got me into trouble once with my parents saying that I had a man in my room last night, so my mom went mad. My boyfriend hadn't been to our house for a couple of days, so my mum asked my sister what did he look like, and my sister said that he was dressed funny and was carrying a candle in a see-through box, which my mum twigged must have been a Lantern. My sister said that he walked through her room into mine. The strange thing was that I always kept my door closed, and when I mentioned this to my sister, she said, "No, he walked through the door." My mum and I just looked at her and said, "Oh OK," when I was really thinking OMG.

Caroline

Till Death Do Us Part

I live opposite some old people bungalows. One night I was woken up and decided to look out of the window. An ambulance was reversing down the road opposite my house, and a lady was stood in the doorway with her husband behind her, his hands on her shoulders. It was a lovely sight, but having known he was very ill, this surprised me. He had died before the ambulance was called and what I saw was him giving his wife support as she waited for help to arrive.

AnonymousThe Man with No Mouth

My three-year-old daughter kept seeing a figure a while ago in our flat; she said that he was dressed all in black, lying on my bed, and that he didn't have a mouth. Several times she said that he was standing at the foot of my bed, and once "with light coming down, down, down" (my daughter's words) from the ceiling, and this was in the middle of the night. She would often creep into my room at night but wouldn't go to my side of the bed for all the bribes in the world. I can tell you I seriously almost had a heart attack when she mentioned that he was lying next to me in bed.

I got her to say, 'please go away because you are scaring me,' the next time she saw him and when she did, he was again at the foot of my bed. There were 'sparkles' on my bedroom door, and they vanished into a teddy (which I then couldn't find all day). This teddy previously belonged to a late friend of mine). I know how ridiculous it sounds, but she hasn't seen the man again.

Claire

Malcolm

When my son and I moved into our new house, which is not far from the German Underground Hospital, I felt that there was someone here all the time. It was only when my son, who was only two years old at the time and could talk very well for his young age, said, "Mummy, a man was talking to me in my room." I said calmly, "Is he a nice man? And what does he look like?" He said, "He was nice."

"That's good," I said, then asked again about what the man looked like. He said, "He had no face".

"Did he tell you his name?"

"Yes, it's Malcolm," he replied.

Now, my son was only two years old, and he had never heard of the name Malcolm before. I know that 100%.

Also, we were in the house with my son's dad when our

son looked over to the corner of the room and said in a surprised, happy little voice, "Hello, Malcolm."

My ex and I just looked at each other and froze and said something like, "Oh my God." This was quite a while ago now, and there has been no more Malcolm. I asked my son if he still sees the man, and he told me, "No." Thank Heavens! All of my friends and family know about Malcolm and take the mick because I told them that I said to Malcolm to go to the light and there will be family there waiting for him. Since then, no more Malcolm. I think that he has gone for good now, and from what my son had said he was nice, so my son wasn't scared of him.

Rachel

My Daughter's Unwanted Visitor

My daughter, who is now three years old, would wake at night scared. She said there was a man in her room, and this went on for a few weeks. Then one night, she woke screaming, saying her teddies were shaking and moving. I would normally have brushed this off as a nightmare, but I had packed away all of her toys neatly before bedtime. I had carried her to bed as she had fallen asleep on the sofa, but the toys were spread all over her room when I ran into her bedroom after hearing her scream. There was no way that she could have messed them up herself; she was asleep when

I put her in bed.

A day or so later, we were out of the house and in a friend's parked car when my daughter insisted that the man from her room was stood in front of our car; no one else could see him. We moved her out of that bedroom, and she has never spoken of the man since, although I now sleep in that room. I have a feeling that someone stands in the doorway watching me. It makes me feel scared to the point that I refuse to sleep on the side of the bed closest to the door. No things have moved since we have had that bedroom. My daughter is very reluctant to sleep in there even with us, although she will occasionally creep in about 6 a.m. and be happy to climb into bed and sleep. My partner is of the mindset that he won't believe it unless he sees it, but even friends and family have been here when strange things have happened and seen strange things themselves.

Anonymous

The Creepy Voice

When I was around four years old, I had an attic conversion bedroom in a house on Vauquiedor Hill. One morning, I woke up because I could hear something calling my name in a really creepy man's voice. I looked around but could see nothing. My family were asleep, so I cried out "leave me alone" and put the pillow over my head. I then had one of those shivery feelings and fell asleep. I woke up later on in the morning, and it was as if nothing had happened. Afterwards, I became obsessed with the idea that my bed covers were haunted, and I never used them again.

Anonymous

Room with a Spook

I grew up on St. Jacques estate (St. Peter Port) from 1978 through the mid-90s and currently live on the estate again. When I was a kid, I used to have the box room at the front of the house, and on a few occasions, I would wake up and see a scruffy bloke sleeping on the other side of the room. I never said anything until I was older when I told my mum about what I saw as I thought that maybe one of their friends was staying over for the weekend. My mum told me that she wouldn't ever let anyone stay over, especially not in our bedrooms, so I had no idea who this guy was that I kept seeing.

When we were old enough, my parents did say that a guy had passed away in the house just before we had moved in. A neighbour had mentioned it to them.

Jon Vokes

Mean Spirited

A flat that I used to live in Vauvert (St Peter Port) was haunted. My brother used to stay on the couch sometimes, and the ghost used to sit on the computer chair by the couch and spin the chair around, hitting the couch. He used to get scared. The ghost also used to sit and talk to my daughter when she was little, and he used to make a lot of noise when she was sleeping. I only got scared once. For some reason, I was drawn to her bedroom when I went in. She was sat on the window ledge about to jump because the "man" told her to follow him this was on the second floor.

My friend who was with me remembers when we were moving into the house, and they were helping us unpack our clothes and belongings, they heard what they thought was me coming in the front door through the lounge and kitchen up the stairs. So, they went to the top of the stairs to look, and there was no one there. Then the footsteps carried on and went past them to the little bedroom, which was the source of all the trouble.

Brenda

The Faceless Man

My daughter had a strange encounter on La Mare De Carteret playing fields (Castel) a few years ago. She saw a strange figure and was understandably traumatised. She gave me a very detailed description saying that the figure that she saw and still describes to this day was a man dressed in a black cloak, top hat, and carrying a long walking stick. He had no face and was very tall. My daughter also commented about the mist coming across the pitch as the man stepped back through the hedge; the hedge didn't rustle or move, which freaked her out even more. This happened about dusk.

I'm an open-minded person but never thought anything much of it again until one night when I was walking my dog around there at dusk. After discussing what had happened with various people, two friends of mine said to have experienced a ghost there many years ago and quite eerily, they gave me a very similar description as to what my daughter saw a few years ago, without me even mentioning her sighting.

After gaining some information from Guernsey Days Gone By, I found out that there were changes to that area in the 1930s, so I googled the dress code for the early 1900s and saw that there is actually a figure on there, wearing almost the same style/long length cloak. This just left me very curious as to what my daughter saw that day.

Anonymous

Unseen Hands

I live on the Chemin de Monts estate (Castel), and a few years back, I had a psychic come round to my house as I had some strange things going on there. One night when I was half asleep, I am certain someone had grabbed my hand. In the morning, this psychic called my friend and asked if I was OK. When my friend came round for a coffee that morning, she told me that the lady had asked about me as she had a dream about me. She said the lady thought it was her grabbing my hand that I had felt the night before.

An hour or so later, the psychic came round to my house and said that she felt something in the house. She then went upstairs, pointed to one of the bedrooms and said, "The naughty one sleeps in here." Yes, the naughty one did! She then went to the next room and told me that this room, which was my son's bedroom, was guarded by an angel. Suddenly, she turned around and started shouting, "Don't you bloody talk to me like that." She said there was a man there and that his name was Tim. She asked him politely to leave as he was unwanted in my house and he started swearing at her. She said they had an argument before he finally left.

Charlotte

Chapter 11 - Haunted Roads And Lanes

Too Close for Comfort

I haven't seen anything for over ten years now, but here are my two incidences that occurred close together. The first was back in 2000; I was walking back home at dusk from town when I could hear two men talking close behind me in a foreign language (sounded Eastern European) as I walked towards the bunker by Hougue a la Pierre (St Peter Port). Opposite the bus Depot, they started getting closer, so I pretended to look towards Herm to get a better idea of who was behind me. I could tell that there were two men over my shoulder; I am originally from Liverpool and was a martial arts instructor, so I like to have an idea who might be a potential threat. Eventually, they got so close that I felt it was an invasion of my personal space, so I turned to face them, and there was no one there. I wasn't frightened but felt shocked and was left with an uncomfortable feeling.

The second experience was in 2001, walking up fountain Street (St Peter Port) at lunchtime. As my office was nearby, I could hear someone walking right behind me to such an extent that they were just too close to me. I made an excuse to turn my head towards the carpet shop so I could size up to my potential opponent when I caught a glimpse of a tramp—like, grey-haired old man in a blue 70s style parka jacket who then just disappeared into thin air.

114

Hugo

A Scary Sight

I was driving my bus up L'Eree Hill (St Pierre du Bois) towards the Longfrie Hotel one evening, and as I got closer to the bus stop opposite the hotel, it was getting dark when I saw a figure pushing a bike from the left towards the pub across the road. He was wearing a long mac type coat. I then saw a car approaching from the airport side towards me and realised that it was going too fast to miss the figure and I expected an accident to happen. I slowed down, but to my amazement, the car carried on and the figure was nowhere to be seen. I was on a bus, so I was high up enough to see.

I wasn't sure of what I'd seen at first. It took me a while to realise that I might not have seen a living person. I can't explain what had happened, but it was very disturbing.

Carolyn

The Ghost Road

I was riding home one night along the Grand Roques Road (the long straight one) when this white blur just appeared in front of me. I had to stop as I thought I was going to crash into it. I opened my eyes after thinking I was going to crash, but nothing was there. Then another couple of nights later, my parents came home after my brothers' parents evening all confused saying that they had seen a blurred figure pass in front of their car along the same road!

Adam

The Strange Late-Night Encounter

Walking home with a friend one night, I saw a tall slim black shadow figure stood on the Fort Road (St Peter Port) pathway. My eyes never left the figure as I moved behind my friend to pass them when they literally disappeared in front of my eyes. My friend saw nothing. I felt that it was a male figure; I didn't take much notice of what clothing etc. they were wearing because I thought that I was just moving out of the way for another person to get past us. It wasn't until they were gone that I realised that they were not another walker.

Judi

A Ghost in the Road

My boyfriend and I were driving past the Chain house one night when I saw someone step out in front of the car. I went to shout out, but we drove right through them, and no one was there when we turned back to check.

Anonymous

Walking Through Walls

About 25 years ago, I was driving up towards Haye Du Puits (Castel) by Saumarez Park when a figure walked straight out in front of my car. It was raining, and I jammed on my brakes thinking I was going to hit somebody, but as I stopped, I watched them walk straight through the wall on the other side of the road. They had a long hooded coat on. Very creepy!

Michelle

The Haunted Road

It was Saturday 3rd January 2015 at approximately 8 p.m. when my daughter was driving along the road L'Ecluse that takes you to St Andrew's Road. She was heading towards the filter as she was picking her boyfriend up from The Last Post. Halfway along that road on the right-hand side (the field side), she saw a figure dart in front of her and go straight into the hedge. There was no opening in the hedge, and the figure was just the torso and head. She said it was a man with a black coat on who darted in a rush, heading towards the Little Chapel. She also said that there were no facial features, but she had never seen anything like it before, and she knew right there and then that she had encountered a ghost.

I've also heard of another friend seeing a ghost girl along that same stretch of road. I know it's supposed to be very haunted in St Andrews and the Talbot Valley way. This freaks me out as last summer, I had walked along that stretch of road on my way back from The Last Post around midnight. Never again!

Anonymous

Haunted Pathway

One weekend I was running at Cambridge Park at about 7:30 a.m. After I ran past the toilet block and towards Les Cotils, I looked across and saw someone on the path that runs parallel to L'Hyvreuse about halfway down. Typical me wondered if they were walking a dog. I turned the corner, and there was no one on the path. All I'd seen was a dark figure on the edge of the path - almost convinced myself that it was a tree or shadow.

Ali

Chapter 12 - Spooky Shops

Things that go Bump in the Night

One encounter I had was in a furniture shop (St Peter Port) doing an overnight ghost hunt with the owner and island FM. Quite a few alarms were rigged around the floors and corridors. Nothing much was happening, so the owner and myself went up into the attic. The attic spanned the whole length of the building and had wooden floors with various items of furniture covered over up there. We sat in a little raised area, and the lady said out loud, "'Come on, let us know you are here" a few times, when suddenly, we heard a humongous bang from the other end of the room. It was like someone had a broom handle and whacked it hard to the floor. She then said something else and this bang happened again, and then all of the alarms on the other floors were set off. We sort of ran to the stairs side-by-side, and when I was nearly at the bottom, I felt a sharp dig in the back of my right knee. I fell down about three steps but got up quickly, and we ran down the three floors to the front of the building where everyone else was waiting.

Julie

The Shoe Shop Ghost

Years ago, I used to work in a small shoe shop by the church in town (St Peter Port). The stock for the shoes was stored in a vaulted cellar underneath. One morning, we opened up the shop and went into the cellar only to see that there were shoe boxes placed all over the floor. None of them was open, so they couldn't have fallen, and all the sizes had been mixed up. This is not the first time that I experienced strange things happening at work; I also worked at another shop in the late '80s where all of the staff and myself had lots of experiences there too.

Nikki

The Spooky Saturday Job

I used to work in one of the shops in town (St Peter Port) when I was a teenager on Saturdays and one of my jobs was to wash up the coffee cups at the end of the day. The space was upstairs in the old storeroom and I always felt uncomfortable up there. One day when I was up, there some of the cups that I had just washed up and started moving on their own. Now I know that sometimes happens because of a wet draining board, but it just wasn't the same sort of movement. This was really aggressive, plus the atmosphere in there felt dark I hated going up there.

Mandy

Spooky Shop Assistant

I used to work in a shoe shop in St Peter Port, which is no longer open, and over the years, I had some strange experiences. One day I was upstairs working in the stock room, and I heard one of my colleagues pulling some boxes out or putting them away in a couple of bays down from where I was. I thought that it would be funny to creep up on her and shout "BOO." Well, I did just that…only that when I jumped out into the bay, there was no one there. I decided to do some work downstairs rather hastily.

Another time, back when stores used to close at 12 o'clock on Christmas eve, a few of us were having a small works party upstairs. The manager, deputy manager, and I saw a shadow pass from the main stockroom to the top of the stairs. It was only seconds, but we definitely saw it, and it wasn't anything to do with the wine.

When I became acting manager in 2015, I would often stay behind to finish up paperwork in the evenings, and I got used to the strange sounds etc. Most of them I put down to sound travel from neighbouring buildings, but on the odd occasions, I felt that I was being watched. I often even heard things like footsteps coming up the stairs, boxes being moved in the fixtures, and even thought on two occasions that my name was being called. I thought it was a member of staff who had maybe forgotten something and had come back into the building but when I went to greet them, no one was there.

The most recent experience I had was a few years ago in the ladies' stockroom downstairs. I went to pull a box of shoes for a customer out of one of the bottom shelves when a box that was properly on the top shelf popped out and just missed my head. This was witnessed by another colleague who was chatting with me at the time.

All in all, there was a lot of strange things, mostly consisting of boxes "falling" off shelves and the sound boxes being moved etc. Also, the tap on the sink in the men's toilet would start running by itself too. This happened a lot, and I used to think that it was one of the guys forgetting to turn it off after washing their hands until I actually witnessed hearing it turn on when no one was in there. Most of the time, I wasn't scared, and I actually gave the "spirit" a nickname: George, and if I did start to get a bit scared, I would just say, "That's enough now, George; you're beginning to scare me," and I can't quite explain it but it was like the atmosphere would change and I would feel comfortable again. I even used to start saying, "Good morning, George," if I was first in in the morning, and saying "Bye, George," when I left in the evenings. I even told "him" when I was leaving for another job and told him to behave.

Tanja

Back from the Beyond

My wife and I went to a retail store (St Peter Port). One afternoon, we were the only customers in there at the time. Whilst talking to the lone salesman, my wife saw an elderly gentleman in a tweed suit and flat cap (1940's working man-style) to her right, but as she turned to look directly at him, he vanished! A moment later, he reappeared, and the same thing happened again! Very strange.

Rachel

Poltergeist Activity

I worked in one of the shops on High Street (St Peter Port), and the basement storeroom and office had a poltergeist spirit that would throw things off the stock shelves and move things in front of the manager while she was working at her desk. It was scary, so they got a priest in to try and get the spirit to move on.

Amy

Chapter 13 - Unexplainable Ghostly Experiences

Ghostly Encounter (not sleep paralysis)

The first time it happened, I was seventeen years old. I woke up with a really uneasy feeling, sensing something was in my bedroom. I was too scared to open my eyes for fear of seeing something that I didn't want to see. I was also physically unable to move; my whole body was paralysed as if there was an unseen pressure keeping me from moving. I tried to call out but was unable to speak. This went on for about five minutes every time it happened, with it becoming quite frequent over the next couple of months.

My bedroom was situated at the back of the house overlooking the L'Islet Dolmen (St Sampson). I always remember having nightmares and issues with sleeping in that back bedroom. In one disturbing dream when I was younger, I recall seeing a red face like the devils in the top corner of the room. I was so scared that I ran to my parents' bedroom, refusing to sleep in that room for the rest of the night. As this dream was so vivid and seemed real, it really frightened me as a child, and I still recall it to this day.

This strange experience of waking up feeling paralysed didn't just occur at my parents' house; one night, I decided to stay over at my grandparents' house in Vauvert (St Peter port) when the same thing happened there. It was as if whatever was doing this to me had followed me there. Yet again, I just couldn't open my eyes to look. I was petrified. The only difference this time was that the bed covers were being pulled as well. I tried to call out to my grandparents, but I couldn't speak or move. After praying for whatever it was to go away, it stopped after a few minutes. I was so scared that I couldn't sleep for the rest of the night.

At that time, I was working in a hair salon as a junior apprentice when one day, a client came into the salon to get her hair done. One of the other girls had been talking to this lady and found out that she was a psychic medium. As the latest occurrence had just happened at my grandparents' house a few days earlier, it was still playing on my mind as to what could be bothering me at night. So, I decided to ask this lady if she knew what it could be and how to put a stop to it.

It turned out I had some kind of spiritual energy attached to me, causing all of these problems when I was trying to sleep. This lady said that she could say a prayer to stop all of this from happening again. So, there we were stood in the upstairs part of the salon where this lady with her hair dye was standing in front of me with two of the other girls that I worked with, reciting a prayer in Latin.

Well, all I can say is that it worked because, thankfully,

this never happened to me again, and I am just grateful that I met this lady who came into the salon that day.

Kate

The Mug Throwing Ghost

I was brushing my teeth one night - this was before we had the extension built in the house. I was in the bathroom where the mirror was by the window, and I saw someone's reflection in the window. I ducked thinking someone was outside throwing something when a mug that I had left in the kitchen was thrown, narrowly missing my head. I turned around and shouted, "What the hell was that!" to my partner, but she wasn't there. She was in the lounge, and shouted, "What you doing?" I said "I have just had a mug thrown at my head."

The house felt haunted when I moved in, and whenever my partner travelled away for work, I hated it as weird stuff used to happen. I would wake up and couldn't turn over; I felt like I was being held down. It was horrible, so I slept with the lights on after that. We have renovated the house, so maybe we disturbed something or made a spirit upset by changing things around. We also came across a really old photograph hidden behind the fireplace, which we thought was strange.

Anonymous

Note: This is the same property where my brother Robert said he saw the shadow standing in the doorway when he went to visit them.

The Thing

We had done the ghost hunt in the German underground hospital a couple of days before this experience happened, so I was already feeling a little bit shaky. Anyway, I woke up from a normal dream and felt that there was something in my room watching me. The rest of my family were fast asleep, so I lay back down and tried to get back to sleep. Just then, though, my cat came into my room and meowed. It stood still by my door, just looking at the same place in my room for ages. I tried to get out of bed to switch on the light when suddenly something sat on my chest and legs; I couldn't get it off. I know it wasn't my cat because it was by my door and during the time, I felt this weight on me, the cat was staring at my bed and after a few minutes, the 'thing' - whatever this was - got off me, and I saw the curtain move as if there was wind coming through the window, but the window was shut. Then the cat stopped meowing and came and sat on my bed next to me. It was so weird.

Anonymous

Chapter 14 - Victorian Ghosts

Conversation with a Ghost

A few years ago, my sister and I were heading home from town. We always used to walk through candy cemetery (St Peter Port) on our way home. I was no more than 13 years old. My sister was 15.

Anyway, I couldn't remember the month, but it was a beautiful hot summer day. It was about 4 in the afternoon as we started to walk in the bottom entrance of the cemetery. As we came up the steps, we noticed a very old man at the top. He was dressed in dark clothing and he was leaning against the granite statue.

We saw that he had this old push pram that was black and white in color and it had big wheels full of old stuff like clocks and other things. However, everything seemed just like new. He looked clean and tidy and had a sturn look on his face. As we walked up to him, he said hello to us. We all spoke for about 10 minutes.

He told us to be good, and we said our goodbyes and walked away. We hardly took 8 steps, and as we rotated back to wave goodbye, but he had disappeared. I think we were more shocked than anything because we didn't hear him move. Surely, we would have heard something at least, bearing in mind that it was a filled old fashioned pram. Also, it was a very flat cemetery, so you could see all around it. We quickly took a look around the cemetery and walked back to the bottom entrance but couldn't see him anywhere. The only way I could describe this man was that he wore a Victorian dress and he had a long white beard ..well, just like Victor Hugo. It was so strange as he was so human in the flesh.

Stan

Victorian Ghost Girl

I saw a ghost when I was working at a shop on the bridge (St Sampson). A few years ago, when I was in the shop basement, she was about ten years old with shoulder-length hair, and she was dressed in Victorian clothes. She was standing by the door just looking at me. When I told my mum, who used to work next door in a shoe shop, she told me that the staff always saw this girl, but mum never said anything until I told her.

Helen

Jane's comments: Helen's story I was not surprised about as when I worked at the shoe shop, different staff would not go downstairs. They always said that it was haunted and the shop that Helen worked at was next door; I had been told that the ghost who haunted the place was a little girl.

The Victorian Lady

A few years ago, I was told a story about a house on Vale Road. The owners always said that it was haunted and that they thought it was a man causing different things to happen in the house. One night, they had friends around for dinner. They were all sitting down around the table having a lovely meal when one of their friends said, "You know your ghost; you always said to us that it's a man. Well, she is standing over you dressed in full Victorian clothing."

Jane

The Funeral Procession

There is a story about a funeral procession that goes around the back of the airport (forest) and comes out by the store in Saint Peters. Someone I knew saw this Victorian procession with a horse and cart many years ago. It was witnessed by a group of young men, who were shocked at the sight.

Alison

Dead Silence

When I was little, I used to live on the Rouge Rue estate (St Peter Port). I remember seeing a little girl in Victorian clothes sitting at the end of my bed. She appeared quite a few times but never said a word. My bedroom was the small box room in the house.

Also, once when I used to play on the estate, the forest behind was accessible, as well as the bunker there. I remember rolling a tyre down the tunnel just for it to roll back up; my friends and I were really scared as we had no idea who or what had pushed the tyre back towards us.

Laura

Chapter 15 - Paranormal Stories Of Haunted Hotels, Guest Houses, And Pubs

The Comforting Ghost

I tell this story as this is part of the Bailiwick; in May 2000, we went for an annual stay in a guest house on the island of Sark. After arriving back from a walk, I decided to have a nap, and my husband went to read his book in the garden. After a short time, I started crying uncontrollably and felt some hands on my leg's gently rocking me back and forth. Without lifting my head, I said, "I am ok; go back down and read your book."

After speaking to my husband about it, I got to know that he had not come up to the room. We mentioned this to the owners and found out that the house was occupied by a ghost in Lederhosen. You see, my father had died only four weeks earlier, and I was vulnerable. The ghost was trying to comfort me.

Claire

The Man in the Hat

My husband ran one of Guernsey's hotels, and one night, my daughter could not sleep, so she came into the bar with us. She said to me, "Why is the man with the large hat behind the bar?"

"Which man?" I asked, and she replied, "The one with a feather in his hat." Then she told me that he always came into her room at night to say goodnight.

I found out that the hotel used to be the Dutch embassy and the man she described fitted the description of an old Dutchman. The guests, as well as us, saw many people walk through the walls in this location.

Jo

The Coffin Man

About four years ago, we stayed at a hotel in Fermain (St Peter Port), and one night whilst staying there, I saw a man appear holding a coffin at the end of the bed. I also heard the sound of glass or bottles clinking as if they were being dragged up the hill. There was no explanation as to what could have caused that noise. I thought it was very strange, and there was nobody else around. I'm used to seeing strange things happen, but this was really weird.

Sharon

The Haunted Pub

The Helmsman Pub (St Peter Port) had a ghost of a little old lady; my nan and a few others saw the little old lady ghost in the pub. One of the houses in Cornet Street was haunted (next to the Helmsman). When I lived there in the early '80s, I never saw it but felt its presence. I also heard it a few times.

Anonymous

I have also seen the little old lady upstairs in the pub; she was dressed in a black dress with a white collar and cuffs with a white apron on; she seemed to be looking for something.

Heather

The Spooky Hotel

My sister and I were put in a hotel in St Martins after being fog stuck at the end of our holiday. As we got to the hotel, I could feel something strange, and I wasn't happy staying there. After a lovely meal, we went to our room and chose to keep the telly and the bathroom light on as we didn't like the feel of the room. During the night, my sister smelled 'aftershave' near her, and a man touched her side. I never slept that night but was awake when she jumped out of bed and turned the TV off, jumping back into bed with the covers wrapped around her. I never saw or smelt anything. I was told by a Guernsey friend that a man had died nearby, which was quite close to our bedroom window. The following morning, we spoke to the ladies that were in the room next to us, and they had heard a funny noise all night in their room. Every time one lady got up to see what it was, the noise just stopped. That was a very strange night.

Anonymous

The Haunted Hotel

This is a 100% true story relayed to me by my sister.

One day in mid-October 2019, my sister and one of her best friends stayed in a hotel on a 'girly' weekend. On the first evening, which was a Friday, after eating downstairs, they went up to the room that they were sharing, watched TV, and had a good natter and catch up. During the mid to later part of the evening, they both heard some noises on the landing outside their room, in the vicinity of their room, and outside their door. She described them as weird bangs, knocks, and rattling noises, but neither of them was brave enough to open the door to see what it was. The noises eventually stopped.

The next morning before breakfast, she asked the receptionist if the hotel was haunted, to which the lady replied that although she had not seen anything herself, other guests had reported seeing and hearing things.

That evening on Saturday, they again ended up in the room talking, and they both heard the same bangs, knocks, and rattling noises on the landing around the same time like they did the evening before. They did not open the door to find out what was making those noises. Again, like the evening before, the noises stopped after a while. They eventually went to sleep - she thinks around midnight. At this point, I should add that my sister's friend is quite deaf in both ears, so she took her hearing aids out to go to sleep.

My sister then said that they were both suddenly woken up at 3:00 a.m. by a mighty crashing or loud bang-like sound from directly above the ceiling in their room, so much so that my sister's friend heard it without her hearing aids in. She described it as extremely loud and as though a wardrobe had been pushed over in the room above them. Then they heard loud dragging sounds as if the furniture was being moved or dragged around the room. My sister also heard distinct muffled voices - mostly male, she thinks - but could not decipher what was being said or any of the words. My sisters' friend could not hear these voices due to her deafness. They thought that the people in the room above were moving furniture around for some strange reason at this ridiculous time. These noises carried on for a while then stopped, but they both went back to sleep, so I cannot say how long the noises lasted.

The next morning before breakfast, my sister went to the reception desk again and said she wanted to make a complaint against the people in the room above them. She told the receptionist what they heard that night at 3:00 a.m., and that she wanted to let them know what the guests above were doing. The next bit shocked them both; the receptionist told them that there was no one above them as there was no room there. Yes, they are on the top floor. Also, that there was no one in the rooms on either side of theirs, they were told that even the cleaners wouldn't go in that room alone.

This freaked out my sister and her friend because my sister instantly knew then that she had witnessed and heard something paranormal that night. There was a void of only three to four feet above their room before the roof.

They went home later that morning after their weekend together, but she said she would not have stayed in that room any longer. She was a sceptic up until this time, but after those two nights there, she totally believes in the paranormal and still talks about it now. I spoke to her about this afterwards, and she said that it was exactly as she described and that these noises were directly above them that night. She has realised that she had heard spirits/ghosts or poltergeists.

My sister and her friend - both mums - would never dream of making stuff like this up; they could just not believe the loudness of the noises.

Tim

Chapter 16 - Dark Figures And Shadow People

Dark Shadows

My wife went to our storage unit (Vale), and as she stood on the second floor at the lift. She looked to the right and saw a person's 'shadow' peering round the corner at her. It then rushed towards her, and at about a metre away, it just vanished. She was terrified! I'm not sure what was there before or if this relates to something being attached to an object, artefact, or Ouija board being stored in a storage room there.

Rachel

Shadow People

I have also seen two shadow people on two separate occasions; they were both peering at me in doorways. One time, this happened in my bedroom about 6 p.m. when I lived at Sandy hook (St Sampson), and another time, it was mid-afternoon when I was visiting somebody's house. They were both full black figures and both took me completely by surprise.

Robert

The Man in Black

One night when I was living at Sandy Hook (St Sampson), I kept drifting in and out of sleep when suddenly I felt weird like somebody was there in the room. I kept looking at the door, and after about the sixth time, I looked up and saw a tall, dark shadow of a full-figured man dressed all in black. He had long hair and was wearing a long dark trench coat. I was so scared I looked away. When I looked back, he was gone.

Anonymous

The Shadow Man

We have a shadow man in my house who mainly appears to me and sometimes to others in our hallway. One night I was asleep and my family said that when they were all sitting in the lounge, the door just slammed shut for no reason.

Lucas

What Lies Beneath

A couple of years ago, my husband - who also works with me - and I drove our car into the car park under our place of work. It was early morning when we parked up, and as I got out of the car, I felt the need to look over to the end of the car park that we had driven in from. That's when I saw an apparition of a female carrying what I first thought was a mug of tea or coffee that was cupped between her two hands. I was thinking, *how strange to bring your drink into the dark car park!*

However, the apparition/figure walked straight through the wall. My husband had no idea what I had just seen, and the weird thing was that I could not tell him as I felt this was so strange. As we walked away, I wanted to look back, but something stopped me from doing so. It made me wonder if it was a candle that the apparition was carrying and not a cup of tea or coffee. I have no idea. Apparently, there have been reports of strange activity in the lower parts of the building. I hear from time to time that some of the older guys who do maintenance work have had a few odd experiences, but none of them have been shared with me.

One weekend I had to go to work due to a heavy workload, and whilst I was logged onto my PC, I felt a presence to my left side. I saw the outline of what I believe was a man. I was shocked, my hair was standing on end, and my breathing was extremely rapid. Well, I have had the odd spooky feeling before, but this was very different. I just cannot explain it. I have been told before that my place of work is apparently built on an old graveyard, so this could be the cause of this strange activity.

Anna

The Spooky Milk Round

It was wintertime around 3:00 a.m. one Saturday morning. While delivering milk in the La Vassalerie Road (St Andrew) going towards the underground hospital, my wife and I were delivering to the houses on either side of the road. We've done the first part of the road and now parked further up she had one house on the left while I had two on the right. There was virtually no wind; it was dry but very dark.

I'd parked outside my second house and so had to go back behind the van to get to the first. The milk at the 2nd house was to the back door, and to get to it, there was a path to the right of the house. There was also a well-established privet hedge about nine feet tall and at least four feet thick between the house prior and the one I was about to go to. As I went to go up the path, I shone my torch in front of me, and as I looked down the path, something went up that path and around the back of that house like a rocket.

I didn't actually see any shape or being, but that hedge bent over to about 45 degrees as though it had been pushed over by something (sort of doing a Mexican wave type thing as it went up the path if you get my drift). It immediately sprung back but scared the life out of me; not only that but as I went back to the van, my wife was sat in the passenger seat, and when I opened the door, she almost jumped out of her skin. She said she had been watching a tall figure standing in the drive of the house on the right about four doors up the road. She could just make out the silhouette in the van's headlights. When I got back in the van, and she looked again, it was gone. A very spooky night that was.

A couple of years later, I jokingly mentioned what I'd seen to my customer who lives in the house opposite the drive in question, and she laughed at me. Apparently, this figure is a well-known feature of the area. She said it was a German soldier. I'll have to take her word for that as I've never seen it since.

Andy

Something in the Corner

When I was younger, I used to keep my pony in one of the stables on the island. I always used to hear strange things, and I always had that feeling that someone was watching me. It was very creepy in those stables, like the way that the stables were laid out. My pony used to refuse to come into the stables and would rear up when near a certain corner in there where you would sometimes see a dark figure watching us, but no one would be there. My pony was the easiest pony to handle ever, so this was unlike him, and I really hated being up there on my own.

My brother also had an experience there where he said it

felt like someone had pushed him off his bike. I hadn't mentioned to him the things that used to happen in those stables, but other people felt the same way about them that it was one creepy place.

Anonymous

The Dark Figure

One day when I was at the hospital and sitting in the ICU department (St Martin), I saw a dark figure that flashed in front of me that had a very vivid face. It scared me a lot and was very strange.

Kylie

Dead Calm

I catch things out of the corner of my eye all the time. I once saw a black shape of a man in my bathroom - no features, just a solid shape. It was weird, and I was intrigued more than freaked out. I peeked at it from around the corner of the door for a few seconds, then went upstairs. It had a calming feel to it more than anything. I didn't feel threatened by it. The house was built around 400 years ago, so it has lots of stories to tell, I'm sure.

Tracey

Paws for Thought

My son showed me our cat lying in one of his clothes drawers one evening. Then when I went to bed, I looked for the cat and checked in his room; I could hear the cat crying, and the drawer was closed. I opened it, and the cat was still inside. He had been there for about five hours. I told my son off for shutting the drawer, and he swore blind that he didn't. No one else would have done it, and he did seem quite genuine. Either he did it absent-mindedly, or we have a poltergeist.

The thing is, when my son was a toddler (he is 13 years old now), he used to swear there were people in his bedroom at night. He also used to suffer from night terrors. Also, about eight years ago, I woke up and saw someone standing next to my bed and when I went to touch them, they disappeared. Then a few days later, it felt like someone was in bed next to me and when I reached out, there was no one there, and my husband was still downstairs. I wondered if I dreamed it, but it seemed quite real to me at the time. We live in an old Guernsey cottage in St Sampson, which dates back to about 1931. Over the years, we have lost things, and then they have turned up in plain view.

Nicola

Chapter 17 - Haunted Homes

Ghostly Footsteps

My husband's family and mine live very close to the L'Islet Dolmen (St Sampson), which is a stone-age burial ground. I was speaking with my parents in law one night, and they told me when their children were young and fast asleep in bed, they quite often would hear the footsteps of a small child running along the landing upstairs.

They would go upstairs to see which one was awake and out of their bed, but when they checked, they were fast asleep. One evening they asked the oldest son, "You go and check," and he thought he would catch one of his younger brothers out, but again, they were both fast asleep in bed.

Stranger still is that their neighbours experienced the same thing in their house and quite often would also hear a baby crying on their doorstep. They would open the door, and there would be no one there. This all stopped in both houses when the children were grown up.

Rachel

That Evil Feeling

When I was living at La Vrangue (St Peter Port), I always had a bad feeling about the lounge. I used to run past it even when the door was shut; it felt like there was something evil in there. It wasn't the same feeling you get when you're just at home alone, and you freak yourself out. There was something bad there.

I've also had nightmares where something was looking at me through the window, and it was evil. I've woken up to my leg being pulled down the side of the bed.

Ellie

Ghosts in the House

I was only nine years old at the time when a few strange things happened in my house. I, my mum, and my sister all heard the ghost of an old man talking. I was asleep in bed one night, and I heard an old man speak in my ear, but he wasn't English. I woke up and felt that I couldn't breathe. I was in shock. I was so scared I screamed at the top of my lungs; my mum ran up the stairs to see what was happening.

The next day, my mum told me that the same thing had happened to her and my sister. Then a few nights after that, I started seeing things in the house. I was going off to sleep when I saw three dark shadows pass my bedroom door (this happened every night). I had the door closed, but at the bottom of my door, you could always see the hallway light on. So, that's where I saw them pass by.

I know that some people won't believe what I have said, but you can ask anyone that I live with about what I saw.

Another time it was my youngest brother's birthday, and everyone was outside in the garden while I was sitting just inside when I saw that there was a little girl at the top of the stairs.

She had a long dress on, and she was in a crouching position. She said, "They are coming," and she looked so scared. I started crying, so my mum came over and asked what was wrong. I explained to her what had just happened seeing that little girl in the house.

The following night my sister's partner was strangled, but there was no one or anything there to explain how or why this happened to them. My mum had this creepy painting next to the stairs, and every time that you would walk past this painting, it felt like it was following you with its eyes. The painting was of a man in an army uniform. In the end, my mum sold the painting at a car boot sale; I wonder if this painting had anything to do with all of the ghostly activity in the house.

After all this had happened, my mum got the house blessed, but one thing that I never understood is why these things always came to me. Maybe because I was young and I had no fear? I don't know, but this wasn't a joke, just very strange.

Latoyah

Ghostly Visitors

Well, I can tell you now the flat where I used to live in St Martins is haunted! I saw so many things when we lived there and I was so frightened all the time. There was a man who I saw a lot and was petrified of. He was very slim, wore dark clothing, and had a really scary face. I felt that he wasn't a very nice spirit if that is what it was. I constantly saw him, whereas more people who came to the flat saw a women spirit. I also used to see the woman, but I felt that she was protecting us.

My stepdad - someone who totally doesn't believe in all of this - thought one time that a little girl ghost had cuddled up to him in bed. Another time my mum saw the same woman spirit as I did, standing up and touching his foot when he was asleep.

Our neighbour told us one day that her young daughter was talking to a woman at night in her room when no one was there, which we thought was strange. There are so many spooky stories to tell about that place, and I would never want to go back there. My mum was told by someone that the male spirit in the house had attached himself to me and that he could be seen in pictures taken of me; they also told my mum that they believed the man wasn't a good spirit.

When the landlord decided to build upstairs (above our

flat), that's when things got worse. Whilst the work was being done, the ghost made its presence clear. We did get the flat cleansed and kept crystals in every room, but nothing really changed. Things still happened. We were told that a previous tenant upstairs had recordings of balls flying across the room and duvet covers being pulled off the bed, but the lady who lived in the property who told us about this didn't seem to feel or pick up on any unusual activity in the flat herself. I'm quite sceptical about it all, like what's real and what's not, but there is no doubt there was something strange going on in that flat.

Anonymous

Ghostly Sightings

We had some strange things happen in a house that we used to live in at St Martins, cupboard doors would open and close by themselves, and a German soldier in a grey uniform and flat cap showed himself in the front bedroom. A little girl dressed like she came from Victorian times often used to sit on the stairs peering through the bannisters at us (which scared my girls to bits). When in the bathroom, the door handle would go up and down by itself, even when I was alone in the house. This really freaked us out.

Also, my daughter kept seeing a black dog running across the back garden. She was only six years old at the time when she told me that it was the little girl's dog that she used to see and hear all of the time. The landlord of the property was aware of this as well and gave us permission to have the house blessed.

Alison

The Running Ghost

I was looking after my mum one afternoon in her house; my husband had popped out to the shop and called me to check that he was getting the correct item. Whilst on the phone in my mum's bedroom below, we heard someone running up the stairs in quite a hurry, and as I looked around, someone ran past the bedroom into the bathroom and slammed the door. Both my mum and I thought that it was my niece and called after her. At the same time that this happened, a jar fell off the shelf in the shop right in front of my husband without any explanation as to how this could happen, which he found freaky at the time. I hung up within about a minute of the door slamming and went to the bathroom to check on my niece. There was no answer, so I opened the door and saw that there was no one in the bathroom. Both my mum and I heard and saw the same thing, and it definitely spooked us out.

Anonymous

Unfinished Business

My story began in 1983. My husband and I bought our first house in the Rohais (St Peter Port). I was an auxiliary nurse at the time; we went to see our new house with our two sons. They were five and eight years old, respectively. We bought the house from the next-door neighbours. It was the lady's fathers house who had died and had left it to her. I went upstairs with my boys and in the front bedroom that overlooked the pub when we all suddenly heard a voice say, "The house is mine." We all ran downstairs, spooked. However, it was forgotten in the excitement of moving in. The boys shared the front bedroom as it was the largest of the two bedrooms.

One night, the eldest child came crying into our room, saying that two men were fighting in his room and that one threw the other down the stairs. We went to his room, but nothing was there, and we saw that his brother was still asleep. My son refused to go back into the room, so much so that we swapped rooms with them.

About a week or so after my brother-in-law and his girlfriend stayed the night, the men slept downstairs, and my future sister-in-law slept with me in my room. My oldest son again couldn't sleep and got in bed with us. He then told us he could see a gun poking out of the cupboard on the left of the fireplace. We couldn't see anything. Then he said that he

151

saw a suit and bow tie hanging up on the cupboard door and he said the bow tie was spinning round. Again, we saw nothing there!

We were friends with the lady next door, and I told her what was happening; it took her a week or so to tell me that the front room was her father's bedroom and that he had once had a fight with his son and had pushed him down the stairs. He had also kept a gun in that cupboard. My husband worked nights, so when he was at work, I was too scared to be in the room alone and kept the curtains open so I could see the people in the pub opposite. We had the whole fireplace wall blocked up in the house and never had any problems after that.

Whilst I was at work one day, someone was telling the people in the staff room about the happenings in a haunted house in the Rohais, so I told them, "That's my house." We ended up moving out three years later.

Carolyn

Spooky Sleepover

I used to live in one of the state's houses for 19 years; there were always strange things happening there, but since I grew up there, I got used to it. My friend and I once saw a figure standing in my room one morning. He was just staring at us and had a black hood up that was covering most of his face.

Another friend stayed over, and someone came into my room, and we both heard it say, "They look so alike when sleeping," when no one else at all was home at the time. So many other things went on in that house. Even before I was born, my brothers and sister had all heard and seen strange things too. My little back bedroom was the worst; my sister had that room before I was born and she used to say that a little girl was in there who she used to play catch with. It used to give my mum chills as when my mum asked my sister to describe her, she said that the little girl didn't have a tongue, so she couldn't speak.

My old dog was petrified to come into that room; she used to bark and scratch the door to get out. My mum also experienced what felt like someone was on her bed that pulled back the covers. Once my mum and I were in the kitchen when we saw a mist-like a figure walk out of the dining room into the hallway. Also, one night, we were in the lounge at the front of the house and we saw a figure walk down the garden path through the front door. We then heard footsteps going up the stairs into the little back bedroom, but when we checked, there was no one in sight, and the front door was still locked.

I never felt threatened living there; I felt that I was being watched at times when I was in my room, and it was always so cold in there. I often used to hear the front door close and footsteps going up the stairs when no one at all was there. I never felt scared as it was my childhood home, but we were definitely not alone in it.

Savannah

Strange Happenings

Footsteps are a common occurrence in houses in the Chemin des Monts area (Castel). I've heard footsteps so many times in my house. I have heard a woman's voice calling my name from the master room, and my mother and I both were like, "What the hell! Who was that?"

Next door to us had a child who was about 3-4 years old at the time, and they used to go on about a hand that used to come out of the attic. Also, in the fields nearby, there is a house that's weird as hell. I've seen stuff happen around that house as a kid, and I've also had friends that have seen weird black figures emerge from the fields whilst we played hide and seek. I have also seen a black shadow in my house once. The list of strange things happening in that house is endless!

Carl

Night Visitors

A friend and I shared a flat along St George's esplanade (St Peter Port). On the top floor, as you went up the stairs, there was a small landing, a bedroom on either side, and a decent-sized bathroom ahead. My room was on the left side of the stairs and always felt like you were walking into a fridge. For the first few nights, my bed was near the front window, but I noticed a cold spot near the end of my bed. I then moved it to the back wall, considering how icy cold it was. You couldn't heat up the room. Even with an electrical fire, you could only warm up the spot in front of it. The room just wouldn't warm up.

A few weeks later, I casually asked my flatmate is he remembered switching off the landing light when he got up to go to the toilet in the night. He said he'd been thinking to ask me the same thing! On a couple of occasions, I was still awake when the light went on, and I would leap out of bed, open the door, and there would be no one around. I also heard someone walking up the stairs occasionally.

In my room, I had two visitors; one was a cat, not one that I'd owned. At first, he used to jump on the end of the bed and kneed its paws before settling down to sleep. I could feel the vibration of his purring, and I could press my foot against him as if he was solid, but I could not see him. Other times, he would jump on the bed by my face, and I would see the

155

indentations from his paws as he kneaded, and I could hear him purr.

The other one was a young girl of about ten years old. She would sit on the end of my bed and sigh heavily. When I watched her, I would see her shoulders slump. One night, she actually sat on my feet. She was like a grey slightly transparent shadow. I would only see her from behind once she had sat on the bed. I saw her maybe five or six times; the other times, as I was falling asleep, I would feel her sit on the end of the bed. I did try talking to her but got nothing. This always happened at night; they didn't seem to be connected and never visited at the same time. I still had the light on one night when the cat jumped on the bed. That was the first time that I saw the paw indentations. I was reading at the time, so I was very awake. The room also had a lot of light pollution, so it was never dark, and you could easily make out everything in the room.

Anonymous

The Ghost Who Didn't Like Noise

When I moved into my new house, my then two-and-a-half-year-old used to see a man in his bedroom. The man used to tell him to stop making noise and stop being loud. He was terrified at first, but then when I was with him, he would say things like, "The man's back." He would laugh

156

and seemed to like him. We actually got someone in, and they asked him to move on. We also had to make lots of noise, apparently. One day my son said, "Man's gone now," and that was that.

Anna

Uneasy Feeling

On one occasion, we were pricing up for some remedial building works to the empty apartments over at a well-known men's clothes shop in town (St Peter Port). When we were taking measurements in the staircase, my colleague heard someone walking around in one of the rooms on the floor above us. He was at the top of the stairs, and I was at the bottom. There was no one else in the part of the building that we were in, and they would have had to get past us to get to the room in question. He was a bit shocked and couldn't manage to tell me until we had left the building. He said he didn't know if I would have believed him. Very spooky!

Bryan

Hands Off

One night when I was working for the civil service doing a night waking duty in a bungalow, I was sitting back on a soft settee about 3:00 a.m. when I must have nodded off for a short while. I woke in a panic feeling with my head almost down by my knees with a clear sense of someone above me holding me down. I struggled and called out when suddenly, I was able to sit up...very scary it was! I never experienced anything there again even though I continued to work there day and night; other staff also confirmed that they had seen and heard strange things there.

Bryan

Disembodied Sounds

I had some strange things happen when I moved into my house a few years ago in La Charroterie (St Peter Port). This one time, I was the only one in the house and I had some music on when I heard a really loud bang followed by a little girl's laugh. Then, it sounded like something was running down the stairs. So, one day, my mum and I decided to ask questions out loud to see if anything happened. We called out, "If there's a spirit here, can you bang three times?" Nothing happened, so we asked again, and we heard three bangs in my bedroom upstairs. We then asked again to make sure, and another three bangs were heard; next, we heard my bedroom door open and close, then there was a loud bang at the bottom of the stairs. We have no idea who or what was causing this to happen.

Carla

The Pope

My mum told me that when we were living at Hauteville (St Peter Port) - I must have been about four at the time - a lot of things used to get moved about in the house. She thought it was me doing it at the time, but I always used to say that it was my imaginary friend who did it. This used to happen a lot and eventually, my mum said she got annoyed with me and asked what does my imaginary friend look like. I described him to be a man wearing pope-like clothes but all black, not white. I also said he had a cane or stick in his hands. Now I know that I wouldn't have known who the pope was at that age, so how could I describe this? Was this a ghost? If so, what did I see as I've never heard of the pope wearing black?

Carla

The Pipe Smoking Ghost

My mum never believed me as a kid, but then she woke up one night to see an old lady standing over my dad and saw the bedroom door opening by itself. I always told her that I used to say see a lady in a bathroom. I also saw lots of other activities and heard strange things too in that house. I used to be petrified and would actually see them, but as I got older, I could only feel them around me. When the houses were being done up, they moved us out a few doors up the road.

159

One day, I was sitting in the living room when I told my mum that I could sense an old man with a pipe opposite me, and she just shuddered when I told her, she was gobsmacked. Apparently, an old guy did live there many years prior (I never knew this) who used to smoke a pipe. I knew he was harmless, and he never did give us any aggro. I felt sad to leave that house, actually.

As soon as we moved back into our house after it had been renovated, that uneasy feeling was still there and all those horrible vibes. Also, walking through the alleyways near the house at night always felt creepy as hell and one particular part I did not like was the area that went to the back car park. It still freaks me out now thinking about it.

Donna

Signs of Paranormal Activity

I live in La Charroterie, (St Peter Port). When we came to view the house, it just didn't feel right. However, it had everything that we wanted and needed. It has always felt as if there is someone here watching us. After a few months of being here, strange noises and things started happening. I'm sure I've seen something out of the corner of my eye at times, and so have other people who have been in the house. There were noises on the baby monitor that sounded like an old man heavy breathing; it was quite croaky! Either my partner or I would check, and my little one would be fast asleep, not snoring or making any sounds at all. Then the floor would start creaking, making a particular noise on a certain spot when you walked on it. We would go and check again, and still, nothing would be there. We used to hear strange noises and movements, and sometimes, it had an eerie feeling about the place. Other times, it was fine.

Then one day it started to get more intense. One morning, I was home alone getting ready for work and thought that my partner had nipped back in as I heard someone downstairs. I went down and as I got to the bottom of the stairs, my cigarettes and lighter just flew off the kitchen worktop.

Following on from this, my eldest child, now three years old, had many experiences. She used to talk to the wall in the corner of the room, laughing and then looking terrified, running towards me and telling me "Man there; now he going upstairs." Sometimes she'd be fine, but the other, very nervous. As you can imagine, this freaked me out; the doors were all locked, so I checked the house, and it was just me and her home.

Over the next few weeks, this became an everyday occurrence. Then one evening while making dinner, my daughter's little play kitchen started moving by itself, and some tins flew off it. The kettle turned on when no one was near it, but my daughter obviously felt something as she came running towards me. My fire alarm has also gone off some mornings for no reason at all, and as soon as I got up to turn it off, it went off only to start again when I lay back down. It almost felt quite intimidating.

The final straw was when I was in my bedroom one lunchtime with my little girl when two separate lots of solid oak drawers, which I can't move as they are too heavy, just tipped over and trapped my little one between them and the bed. They were so heavy I could not free her, so I had to scream for my partner, who was downstairs, to help me lift them. The TV, vases, and lamps came flying off too. Thankfully, she was ok - just very shaken and understandably so. And so were we!

I thought my husband had come downstairs one evening, So I started talking to him and was annoyed that I didn't get a response. I looked, and he wasn't there. He hadn't been anywhere near me. We have heard a few different noises again around the house, but nothing has made us feel too uneasy. My husband has never believed in anything paranormal, but he is certainly puzzled about some things that have gone on in the house. I have always seemed to have some sort of belief in these things, more so now than ever. I decided to call somebody about this for some advice, and they have advised picturing my daughter with light (a bubble of light) around her to keep her protected from evil as young children tend to attract all sorts of energies. They also asked us to speak out loud and say, 'whoever you are, leave.' It seems to have worked. I have no idea why or what happened, but I feel so much happier, safer, and not on edge. Whatever it was has hopefully gone for good.

It went quiet for a while, but since my youngest was born nearly four months ago, things are starting to happen again. I have seen this shadow figure out the corner of my eye again, so we will wait and see!

Donna

The Haunted Apartment

I lived in an apartment in Vauvert (St Peter Port) that was haunted. Past tenants that I spoke to all agreed there was something nasty in there, but for us, it wasn't nasty, just mischievous. We'd get up in the morning, and our keys would be hidden. My smoke alarm would go off in the middle of the night, even when it had a flat battery. My son was a toddler at the time and was always looking at something in the hallway, chattering away to it when we saw nothing there.

Sandra

The Haunted House

I was bought up in a haunted house without a doubt; I now live right next door to it. The house was an unhappy house, and I don't really have any fond memories there, to be honest. My bedroom door was old and used to stick for years, but I, my mum, and my brother had the knack of opening it the first time without it rattling. One night I was awoken by the very obvious sound of someone or something trying to open the bedroom door, which was really shaking, but whatever this was didn't have the knack to open it. I froze, to be honest, and fell back to sleep. I asked my mum and brother in the morning if it was them that was trying to get into my room and they both said that they had not been up in the middle of the night trying to open my bedroom door. I knew it wasn't them, though. I was freaked out.

Another time, I was woken up as my wrist was being grabbed and squeezed, then nothing. It just stopped, which was really strange. Also, when I was alone in the lounge one day, I heard "Pssssttt" really loud. It really frightened me.

Things regularly went bump in the night; both my mum and brother heard heavy breathing by their headboards and by the bedroom door on more than one occasion. I used to see small black cloud-like shapes from the corner of my eyes. I always believed that it was one of our deceased pets, so I wasn't scared of these images at all. I used to be petrified walking down the stairs, though, as I believed that someone was behind me.

In the '60s, a relative of mine lived in that house, and he sadly passed away young from illness in there. He had a bed made up in the bay window where sadly he died. A neighbour's little boy has witnessed seeing a man in the bay window. That house just had bad vibes and was a very unhappy house. There was definitely evil in there; loads of negative stuff went on in that house. I was told by one of the neighbours that these houses are built on an old cemetery.

Anonymous

The Old Farm House

Our old farmhouse in the Rouge Rue (St Peter Port) was definitely haunted. We had some strange experiences there. Once I had my toes and hair pulled, got pushed down the stairs, and my mum got held down in her bed by something unseen. When I was younger, my nan stayed over one night and whilst staying in my room, she got woken up by a little girl crying at the end of her bed. She turned on the lamp as she thought that it was me, but no one was there, and I was still fast asleep in bed. We had a touch lamp in my parents' room and guaranteed it would turn on at the same time every afternoon after we had moved house. We took the same lamp with us, but it has not done this in the new house. We heard a few strange stories about the old farmhouse that a man chucked his wife from the attic stairs, and she fell and hit the flagstones below, dying. We also heard that a small child had died there; we are not sure if there is any truth in these stories, but my dad and I would not sleep in the house alone, and my dad isn't easily spooked. My mum, on the other hand, loved it.

Biennea

The Lost Souls

Over the years, there have been many sightings by my family. My nan used to live in Croute Havilland, and so we would often walk back home to St Martin's along the Fort Road at night rather than go through the lanes. She always told us to watch out for the other people, and we always thought that she meant live ones, but no. One day, (when I was a teenager) she explained that there were lots of lost or remaining souls around there and that none were there to hurt but just to keep an eye. Also, according to my nan, a few of these lost or remaining souls who walked around Fort Road and Fort George were there to keep us safe.

Years ago, my gran used to clean a couple of houses in the fort; she didn't believe in the paranormal, but she did tell me that she knew people who had seen strange things in some of the houses up there, and she herself had experienced something strange when cleaning once in one of the houses up there. One day, she thought that the owner had come home early, so she turned and said "hello" to a man who she then realised was dressed in a strange uniform. She watched him as he then vanished around the corner of the kitchen wall. When she mentioned this to the owner, they told her, "Oh yes, he visits us from time to time; we aren't sure who he is, but he never stays long!"

Clare

Ghostly Conversations

I'm sure that my old house at La Vrangue (St Peter Port) was haunted as I would hear voices downstairs in the lounge of someone talking. One time when it was quiet, I was upstairs one evening when I heard my front door open (it was locked at the time). When I heard someone walk up to my stairs, I went onto the landing to see who it was, but nobody was there. It did scare me at the time. Most times, it didn't bother me as I got used to it; whatever it was seemed friendly enough. After I had moved out, I spoke to the person that moved into my old house, and they said that they heard strange noises and people talking. That house is definitely haunted.

Chezz

Who's Behind the Door?

One experience that I had was when I was living in a ground floor flat in Trafalgar Road (Vale). It was a really hot sunny day and I was doing some housework in the lounge while my daughter, who was about three years old at the time, was in her bedroom playing. Out of the corner of my eye, I saw someone run down the hallway from the bedroom to the kitchen and then slam the kitchen door. I called out my daughter to get out of the kitchen as I'd just mopped the floor; she then shouted back, "I'm not in the kitchen," so I went into the hall and could see light under the door frame. There were shadows that looked like someone was standing behind the door. I tried to open the kitchen door, but it was as if someone was sitting against it. So again, I called out to my daughter, "Get out of the kitchen. I can see you're in there." She then walked out of the bedroom behind me. I was then able to open the door fully and saw that no one was there!

Anonymous

Unexplained Sounds

I lived at La Vrangue (St Peter Port) with my parents and brother when I was about 9-10 years old. I experienced some strange phenomena, including the sound of a sort of crackly breathing and groaning noise in my room and at the top of the landing. Also, I felt something sitting on my bed at night-time. My bedroom had random cold spots in it, even though the chimney ran through my bedroom. So technically, it should've been the warmest room upstairs. I used to find items in my bedroom had been moved, often blaming my brother when he was not even in the house! This one time in my room, I heard the scary breathing sounds and my hair was pulled. I screamed for my dad at the time; he came sprinting up the stairs, and he also heard the weird breathing sounds but to save me from my fears, he insisted that it was the sound of our immersion heater and the hot water pipes.

He later admitted that he could not identify the noise and that the immersion heater was off at the time. Unbeknownst to me, my mum was experiencing a similar phenomenon, and eventually, my parents got a priest to come to our house and have it blessed/exorcised. The phenomenon stopped after that.

Anonymous

More than One Spirit

My uncle (who has since passed away) owned a house that he rented out and it was definitely haunted. My mum and I visited the house to try and move the spirits on. I remember that there was the spirit of a German soldier in the sitting room, and you know that he was there due to the smell of cigarette smoke. There was also the spirit of a little girl in that house that would appear holding a teddy bear.

Hannah

The Spooky Mansion

One night a few friends and I had driven up to Fort George (St Peter Port) to see if we would experience anything strange. We had heard that some parts were eerie and that there was an abandoned house where the back of it had been taken off, but it had never been demolished, which I also found very strange.

On the first night, all but one of us were too scared to go anywhere near the house because it was scary, and it was about a 300ft walk to the actual building. One of my friends was walking with his torch on, and as he swiped the torch across the grounds, we all saw a figure standing next to him. We were all spooked and ran to the car when we all heard footsteps circling around the car and when my friend tried to start the car, it stalled.

The next night we all decided to go back to the house as we were all feeling brave, and we all went round to the back of the house (the part that had been taken off) where you could actually get inside the house through the back door. Two of my friends went into the house while I stayed outside with a friend as we were too scared to go inside. Next thing we heard was the loudest bang coming from the top floor of the house. Suddenly, a light turned on in the opposite side of the house where my friends were at, they both ran out screaming, and as we were all running back to the car, the back door of the house slammed shut really loudly.

When we got back to the car, one of our friends that had stayed in the car when we had gone over to the house told us that they had heard footsteps pacing around the car (this person was not with us the night before when we heard footsteps, so they weren't aware of this). The car also stalled again when we tried to leave. This was definitely not our minds playing tricks. I genuinely felt afraid for my safety, and I felt like I was being watched; we all felt so uneasy there. Something definitely didn't want us there. My friends who went in were petrified; it was the scariest experience of my life, and I will never go back there again.

Anonymous

A Haunting Time

Living at Sandy Hook estate (St Sampson), my daughter and I used to hear footsteps running up the stairs, or a sound like the front door had been opened and shut. I remember my daughter ringing me. She was in the bath at the time, and she asked if I'd just walked in the house, I said "No, I'm still out." She said, "I have just heard the door open and close and someone coming upstairs," but there was no one there. Also, lights would flicker, and photos fell off the wall. I used to blame it on the Dolmen spirits. Oddly enough, we don't hear the noises anymore.

Libby

Signs of a Haunted House

When I was very little and lived on the old Grand Maison Road (St Sampson), my mother told me that I was always chatting to a little boy called David (which I don't think is anything unusual for children to have imaginary friends), but my sister also said that she'd hear scratching on the bedroom wall. She said would come in and see that I would be fast asleep. The house was apparently in the paper after we moved out for being haunted.

Laura

Restless Spirits

I've lived in the same house now in the Vale for 24 years (living here since I was two weeks old). I used to live here with my other three siblings, and we have experienced countless weird goings-on. There are a few things that stick in my mind like when my radio's volume would just suddenly turn up without anyone touching it, and the kettle went on randomly. Also, my brother and I had the same experience of being chased up the stairs of a night time and cupboard doors swinging open on their own. Then one of the scariest things happened going back a fair while ago now; mum and I were sat in our lounge watching TV; we were all calm just chatting when we heard a seriously loud bang on the lounge door that was closed. So, we went out to look, but nothing had moved or fallen over, and nothing could be found to explain what had caused the loud noise.

We were really shaken up, so we decided to get a priest in. He said that he could definitely sense something, so he blessed the house. All was fine for a while, but now I can't help but shift this uncomfortable feeling of being watched almost on a daily basis and having that weird feeling on being on edge all the time. I hear footsteps on my bedroom floor directly above my lounge and when I walk from room to room, the feeling intensifies and then suddenly the temperature drops. On one occasion, my friend and I were chatting in my kitchen; then, out of nowhere, she felt like she got a slap around the back of the head.

Jo

Spooks Everywhere

A house that I used to live in when I was younger at Rue de la Perruque (Castel) years ago had some strange goings-on. I remember that there was an attic hatch in my bedroom that I would hear noises coming from it, and also, the built-in cupboard that was in the bedroom felt strange; I always had the feeling of being watched. It felt really uncomfortable. One day, I left the front door unlocked whilst I popped over to my mate's house for a cuppa, I came back home, and I had been locked out of the house, but the key was inside the door and locked. My mum lives in that house now and has experienced lots of activity there now.

I now live in the Bouet, and not just myself, but my husband, daughter, and my oldest son have all seen shadows of people in the house. We also see flashes of light like a camera flash and also get flashes of colour that appear around the house. A man's voice has been heard throughout the property, too, and things get moved about, especially in the kitchen and the lounge areas.

Tracey

The Bright Circle of Light

I used to live in Hauteville (St Peter Port), and I was convinced that my flat was haunted. We had many experiences there of taps turning themselves on. The shower also used to turn on by itself with no explanation. My child was a new-born, and every time I used to put him down for a nap, I would lie down myself, and this clicking noise would start. I would open my eyes, and it would stop...close my eyes, and it began again. This kept going on. I searched the room but could never find anything. It would never be heard when my eyes were open, which really did freak me out.

We had a small walled-in dark courtyard; I had a cigarette out there late at night. It was pitch black, and from the right-hand corner, this small but super bright circle of light slowly moved diagonally to the left, went brighter, then just disappeared. I told my partner about this, and he then said, "I had seen the same thing but didn't want to tell you as I might have scared you." I'm guessing that it was an orb.

I used to feed my baby in the middle of the night in the lounge in silence and always felt a presence; there was just something that was not right. I used to always be looking over my shoulder. It was always a very cold flat, and the more I think about it now, I feel the place never felt homely or comforting.

Jacinta

Chapter 18 - Guernsey's Myths, Legends And Folklore

Black Dogs

Guernsey has had many different sightings of black dogs over the years; seeing these dogs usually described as being very large with fiery red eyes is said to be an omen of death or bringing impending bad luck upon the viewer. These black dogs are known by different names according to where the sightings have been seen throughout the various parishes of Guernsey. Many of these huge black dogs are said to trail chains behind them and have been seen down dark, quiet lanes late at night, ominously appearing in front of you. Some might follow you, whilst some might just stand there, growling at and watching you. Sometimes the dog is headless and just the sound of dragging chains can be heard. If you come across any of these demon dogs on a dark night, their haunting presence would in no doubt fill you with dread.

La Bête de la Tour (The Tower Beast)

It is said that this dog makes no appearance. It can only be heard on Tower Hill with the sound of rattling chains as the beast passes by. The tower beast supposedly roams around this area of St Peter Port during the winter months and especially becomes more active around Christmas time.

It is believed that if you are unfortunate enough to hear the La Bête de la Tour chains rattle, it is a sign that something bad will happen.

Tchico - the Ancient Dog of the Dead

Tchico is known to be a headless dog that is rumoured to be the phantom of a past Bailiff Gaultier de la Salle, who was hanged in 1320. Supposedly, Gaultier de la Salle had sought after a field that belonged to his neighbour Massy. Gaultier de la Salle then offered to buy the field but was refused; this made him very angry, so he accused the neighbour of stealing two silver cups from him, the bailiff. It is said he had taken and hidden them himself in a nearby haystack. When the deceit was found out, it was Gaultier de la Salle that was sent to the gallows.

This huge headless dog is said to prowl along the Ville-au Roi on moonless nights; those people who have come across the Tchico are said to have tried to hit it with sticks, but the sticks go right through it.

Tchen Bodu

This large black demon dog that is claimed to haunt the area of Clos du Valle, is described as having jet black fur has snarling teeth and has fiery red eyes. Legend has it that if you came across this haunting hound, its appearance foreshadows death for either the witness or for someone close to them.

"La Bête de la Devise de Sausmarez a Saint Martin"

A large black dog is said to haunt the avenue near Sausmarez Manor; not much is known about this phantom dog, though. Some people believe that it roams this area at night to protect the property's boundary.

La Bête du Galet (The Beast of the Shingle)

The beast that haunts the beach by Fort Sausmarez is said to be so horrendous that when it is seen. People stare in shock, remaining immobilised to the spot.

La Rue de la Bête (The Beast's Road)

This beast is said to haunt people walking alone late at night down a lane situated in St Peters. This lane is known as 'the beast's road.' The beast is said to be described as very large - the size of a calf but looking like a dog, and is black. The beast is reported to follow people down the lane, yelping whilst walking beside them. If you are unlucky enough to set eyes on the La Rue de la Bête, legend says that you will die shortly afterwards.

The Fairy Ring

The Fairy Ring situated at Pleinmont is a circular ditch cut into the grass with a flat grassy area in the middle surrounded by large stones. It is also known as the Table des Pions. According to local legend, it is said that if you walk around, it three times and make a wish, the fairies will grant your request, and your wish will come true. In Guernsey folklore, it has been said that the fairy ring has been used as a meeting point for fairies and elves to dance around the stones late at night. It is also where witches would gather to meet the devil.

Witchcraft

Guernsey has many stories about witches, with Le Catioroc being known as a place for witches to meet every Friday night at midnight. And according to folklore, the devil would make an appearance in the form of a black goat. The goat would sit on the centre capstone of the Le Trepied Dolmen, whilst the witches would sing and dance as they worshipped it in ceremonies known as 'Le Sabat des Sorciers.'

The Faeu Boulanger (Rolling Fire) Will O' the Wisp

The Faeu Boulanger is said to appear as an atmospheric ghost light, and according to legend, these lights are the wandering restless spirits of the dead. In Guernsey, the Faeu Boulanger is believed to be a lost soul. A light that has been seen in several different parishes. It is said that if you encounter this ghostly light, in order to stop it in its tracks or to make it disappear, you should turn your coat or cap inside out or stick a knife into the ground with the blade facing up as the Faeu Boulanger will then attempt to kill itself. It will ignore you and attack the blade instead.

The Devil's Hoofprint (Le Pied du Boeuf)

The tale of the devil is said to date back to the early Middle Ages when the devil took up residency on the island of Guernsey. As his presence was not wanted on the island, a Christian saint was sent to Guernsey to expel the beast. A great struggle broke out, and they fought each other across the island, ending up in the northernmost point overlooking Fontenelle Bay. The unnamed saint won the battle and demanded that the devil should flee the island immediately. As the devil turned and leapt north, heading towards Alderney, he left a hoof mark behind imprinted into the rock.

The Guernsey Lily

One beautiful sunny day, the king of the fairies arrived in Guernsey at Vazon in his boat and went ashore. He felt tired after his journey, so he decided to lay down under a hedge to sleep. A pretty young girl called Michele was walking past when she noticed him sleeping; she stopped to take a closer look and saw that his clothes looked unusual. He was wearing strange green clothes and had a green plumed hat; he was very handsome.

Suddenly he opened his eyes and saw Michele standing looking at him, he got up and introduced himself as John. He knew at that moment that he had fallen in love with this beautiful girl. He persuaded Michele to leave Guernsey to go and live as his wife and queen of the fairy kingdom with him, but Michele felt guilty for just leaving without saying goodbye to her parents, so she asked John if she could leave something behind for her family as she knew that they would be upset and would miss her terribly and she didn't want to be forgotten. The fairy king handed Michele a bulb, and she planted it near the edge of the beach, and they left the island on his boat to sail to his homeland.

Soon afterwards Michele's mother came to look for her, and when she couldn't find her, she feared the worst and started to cry. As her tears fell, they landed on the sand and soil where her daughter had planted the bulb. All of a sudden, a beautiful red flower sprung through the soil. It was covered in gold fairy dust, and when she picked this magnificent flower, some of the gold dust blew into her eyes. Instantly, she could see that her daughter was safe, happy, and well. She knew at that moment that Michele would never return back to Guernsey.

On John and Michele's return to the fairy kingdom, all of the other fairies were in awe of the fairy king's new wife, and they all became jealous and wanted a wife just like Michele, thus leading to the fairy invasion of Guernsey.

The Fairy Invasion of Guernsey

The fairy men in the kingdom all decided that they too wanted Guernsey girls as wives after seeing the king and queen living happily together, and so the great fairy invasion began. The fairies left the kingdom to travel to the island to find themselves brides; they arrived in Guernsey in a great horde and made their way across Vazon.

A local man who was tending to his cattle down on the west coast of the island caught sight of the fairy warriors as they emerged from The Cave Le Creux es Faies; they took the frightened man prisoner and told him that they had come to Guernsey to claim the local women as their wives. However, they agreed to let him go so that he could go and tell all of the other Guernsey men their purpose.

When word got around the island, the local men armed themselves and marched to face the fairy warriors. A fierce battle began, and the Guernsey men were defeated. So much blood was shed from the locals and the fairies that the roads ran red with blood in St Peter Port. Today this road is known as La Rouge Rue (The Red Road).

The fairies had achieved what they had come for and took the local women of Guernsey as their wives. They settled down for many years of happiness, but it was not to last as the fairy kingdom called upon the fairies to return back home, leaving their wives and children behind. Folklore says that the mixing of fairy blood with the islanders is the cause of shortness in height for Guernsey people – the descendants of the fairies.

The Fairies' Bat

One day, two well-known fairies on the island of Guernsey who went by the names of Le Grand Colin and Le P'tit Colin were playing a game of bat and ball. For their game, they used a huge stone as a bat that was over four metres long, and they used a huge round boulder for the ball. Even though the fairies were small in size, they had otherworldly strength and regularly enjoyed playing this game on a flat field near the Paysans.

On one particular day, it was le Grand Collins turn for

batting. When he hit the stone ball with such strength, the ball landed beyond the boundary. La P'tit Colin was not happy about this as he was both bowling and fielding. He, therefore, stated that the ball was out of bounds. Le Grand Colin became so enraged that he threw down the giant stone bat and refused to play the game anymore.

The huge stone still remains in its upright position today and is known by local people as La Longue Rocque; it is said that the large round boulder that the fairies used as their ball can be found on the far-away hillside off to the west of the Imperial Hotel.

Le Coin de la Biche

There was a well-known farmer called Henri Mauger that lived in St Martin's at the turn of the nineteenth century, after spending the day down the beach at Saint's Bay with some of his workmen collecting seaweed in their cart to take back to put on the fields, they decided to leave at sunset and made their way back to the farm.

The cart was heavily laden with seaweed and had to be pulled up the hill from the beach by horses and oxen. Back then, the lane was steep and rocky with a deep channel with water that flowed back down to the sea. On each side, tall trees and high hedges lined this walkway until they reached the top of the hill and turned into the corner of the next lane known to locals as Le Coin de la Biche, now known as La Rue des Grons. The place has had a reputation for being haunted by an apparition of an extremely large nanny-goat with large red eyes.

As the men were walking, one of the men said, "Do you think we will see the goat?" Henri then replied, "If we see her, she will not harm us." Suddenly appearing out of the dark narrow lane, an enormous nanny-goat raised up onto its hind legs and placed its forelegs against the back of the cart. Everybody was in complete shock. The animals were frightened and panicked. With all of their strength involved, they still could not move the cart forward whilst this huge beast kept its cloven hoofs firmly placed on the back of the cart.

Realising that they were unable to move the cart, the men frantically unfastened the animals and made a hasty retreat back to the farm away from the nanny-goats glare, thus abandoning the seaweed filled cart in the lane. The following morning, Henri and his men anxiously returned to the lane to retrieve what they had left behind. There was no sign of the goat that they had seen the night before, and surprisingly, they were able to move the cart using just one horse and one ox.

The Fairy Changeling Baby

There once was a young newlywed couple who lived down by the coast at L'Eree. The man's wife was pregnant and shortly after gave birth to their firstborn. One day, the young wife was doing her daily household chores and cooking some fresh limpets on the kitchen fire whilst her husband was out gathering seaweed and shellfish from the nearby beach when all of a sudden, she heard a voice from where her baby was sleeping in the cradle. The voice then said, "I am not from this year or the year before, and not yet of the time of King John, but in all of my life, I never imagined that I would see so many cooking pots boiling!"

Hearing this strange voice coming from the cradle shocked the young mother as she knew that the voice did not belong to her baby, and nobody else was in her home. She then realised what must have happened: a fairy mother had crept into the house and swapped her baby for a fairy changeling.

The young mother had heard some of the older locals talking about fairy changeling babies, so she knew what had to be done. She went over to the cradle and picked up the changeling baby. She walked over to the fireplace and threatened to throw it into the fire. The changeling started to let out high-pitched shrieks. The young mother knew that this would attract the attention of the fairy mother, who suddenly appeared from some bushes just outside of the house. She sprang through the half-open kitchen door and snatched the changeling baby from the woman's arms. She returned the women's own child back into the cradle, turned, and jumped with her changeling baby back through the kitchen doorway never to be seen again.

Spirits of the Dead

In Guernsey folklore, the ancient standing stones, menhirs, dolmens, and megalithic sites that are dotted all over the island are said to hold supernatural powers. Spirit guardians of the ancient dead were said to roam these sites, protecting them from being destroyed by treasure hunters.

Artefacts that were left behind from the past have been found buried around and in these ancient stone structures, which then led locals who were unable to make ends meet search for treasures and objects to sell. These spirit guardians could make themselves appear in many different forms to scare away anyone brave enough to disturb these sites.

One day, a local man who lived on the west coast of the island was in desperate need to provide for his family. He had overheard a conversation about some buried treasure located at the foot of a dolmen that was near Rocquaine Bay, so later that night, he set out to try and find this treasure that would solve all of his money problems if found. He started to dig with his spade for many hours. Night turned into the early morning and finally, just as the sun was starting to rise, his searching paid off. There at the bottom of the hole was a giant ancient pot filled with glistening gold coins.

Nevertheless, as the man stood transfixed at this magnificent find, the gold coins transformed before his eyes into worthless old limpet shells. The worst was yet to come, though; suddenly, an enormous black conger eel appeared inside the dugout hole, its huge body twisting and turning vigorously around the ancient treasure-filled pot. Its giant head raised up showing its razor-sharp teeth, fixing its stare with glaring red eyes on the terrified man.

The man was scared witless; he backed away and ran all the way home, scared for his life, with the treasure remaining guarded and safe in the ground.

Madame Mahy

Long ago, the poor local women in the parishes would take on extra jobs, such as laundry washing, to make more money for their families. The washer-women would work in different houses and quite often overheard the local gossip whilst working away. These women would talk and exchange the gossip which they always kept amongst themselves as if this talk was to be heard by anybody else, including the people that they worked for, their livelihoods, and reputations would be at stake.

One day, regardless of how careful the washer-women had been, a group of the women who worked in the higher up parishes gossip got them into a whole lot of trouble. They couldn't understand how their conversations had found their way back to the people who employed them.

The women talked amongst themselves to try and find out who had gone behind their backs and repeated what they had been talking about in private. After much discussion, they found out that it was the old sea-captains wife, Madame Mahy, who had got them into trouble, but they found this rather odd as Madame Mahy did not employ any of these women to clean her laundry; how could she possibly overhear any of the conversations?

One of the younger washerwomen in the group grew suspicious about this situation and suddenly remembered that every time the group had met up, that there had been a cat sitting in the corner of the room. The unusual thing was that none of the women owned a cat, but somehow the cat would always appear without fail to listen and watch the washerwomen gossip close by. The young woman who had become suspicious suspected that something otherworldly was going on, and so she devised a plan.

The following week, the washerwomen met up one evening as usual to discuss the latest gossip, and yet again, the cat made an appearance too. They were all sitting around the fireplace when the young washerwoman silently picked up the fireplace poker and put it into the flames to heat up. Then, as quick as she could, she grabbed the poker and pushed it onto the cat's nose. The cat jumped up and let out a high-pitched screech, running as fast as it could out of the door into the dark night. None of the other women could understand why the young woman would do such a thing, especially after she refused to tell them why she had done it.

The next morning, word got around that there had been an unfortunate accident. Madam Mahy had fallen asleep in her chair the night before in front of the kitchen range, and half asleep, she leaned forward and had burnt her nose on the hot grate. Then all became clear. The young washerwoman's plan had worked. It revealed that Madam Mahy was a Guernsey witch that had turned herself into a cat on many occasions to eavesdrop on all of the washerwomen's gossip. Madam Mahy learnt her lesson never to do that again.

The Wizard Of The West Coast And His Books Of Dark Magic

Long ago, there was a man called Mr Sarre who lived on the west coast of Guernsey. He had a reputation for being a wizard who used books of dark magic and spells. Some of the local people in the area and some of his neighbours had claimed that they had been afflicted by Mr Sarre's wizardry.

The pastor of the parish of Torteval one day decided to try and resolve Mr Sarre's sinful ways. So, he visited the wizard several times over the weeks, spending hours on end determined to try and convince the man how practising black magic could cost him his life and soul, and that this was the work of the devil. Upon hearing this, the wizard became frightened and realised that he had to change his ways. He decided there and then that he had to get rid of the black books.

Unexplainably, from the time that the pastor had begun his attempt to help Mr Sarre, a mysterious black cat had appeared; it would follow the wizard, watching him day and night everywhere that he went. No matter what he tried, he just could not get rid of the cat. It was impossible to get this animal to leave. Fear crept over him that the cat had been sent by the devil to keep an eye on him, and he was afraid that the cat would attack the pastor in order to take his soul.

The next evening when it was dark, Mr Sarre took the books from his house and walked down to the beach until he came to the low tide mark in the sand. He then started to dig a big deep hole and placed the books inside of it, covering it up with sand. The tide was coming in, and the seawater started to cover the spot where Mr Sarre had buried the black books. He let out a sigh of relief as he watched the shallow water glistening in the moonlight. As he walked slowly back home, he felt like a great weight had been lifted off his shoulders, and he was finally glad to be rid of those books.

When Mr Sarre returned home, he opened the door and walked into the kitchen. He stood still in shocked silence; his jaw dropped. He could just not believe what he was seeing: there sat in a pile on the kitchen table were the black books that he had just buried down the beach under the sand. Furthermore, sitting right beside them was the black cat with one of its paws placed on top of the books.

No one knows for sure what happened to Mr Sarre after that night. His neighbours said that he started acting weirdly and seemed very depressed. He would always be seen just wandering around the cliffs and beaches, until one day when he just disappeared without a trace, never to be seen again. There was gossip that he had thrown himself off the cliffs down at Pleinmont, but some locals believed that he had been succumbed by the devil due to the use of his dark magic.

L'Islet Dolmen, St Sampson's

The German Underground Hospital

The German Underground Hospital

The German Underground Hospital

The Mirus Battery

The Fairy Ring

The Catioroc (Le Trepied)

The Catioroc (Le Trepied)

196

Fort Grey

Fort George

Guernsey Lily

The Lovely Old Lady

Fauxquet Valley at Night

Fauxquet Valley

Castle Cornet

Vale Castle

The Witches' Seat

The Devil's Hoofprint

The Fairies' Bat

Le Creuxes es Faies

Chapter 19 - Guernsey History

L'Islet Dolmen, St Sampson's

The L'Islet Burial Chamber (Dolmen) was first discovered and excavated by La Société Guernesiaise in 1912. This site at Sandy Hook is thought to be dated from around 2000 BC due to the type of pottery that was found and compared with other similar archaeological sites. Findings of pottery and flint were uncovered at this site, but no burials were found here. This unique structure, which consists of a 'Cist-in-Circles' layout, appears to be local to the Channel Islands. The dolmen is situated in the centre of a large stone circle which has four smaller circles adjacent to it, each with a small stone cist in each of the circles.

German Underground Hospital, St Andrews

The German Underground Hospital is the largest remaining structure on the island of Guernsey from the time of the German occupation. These underground tunnels cover an area of about 6,950 square metres (75,000 square feet). Formed out of solid rock, it was constructed by slave labourers of numerous nationalities between the years of 1940 and 1945, many of whom died during the construction of this underground maze of tunnels. One accident that happened killed six Frenchmen during a rockfall, and an accidental explosion killed a further seventeen labourers. The workers used drills, explosives, hand tools and even their bare hands to carve out these tunnels made from solid rock. The German Underground Hospital was first designated for use as a shelter for a partly motorised machine-gun company. Later on, it was decided to be converted into an underground hospital.

The Batterie Mirus, St Saviour

The Mirus gun battery, with its four 30.5cm naval gun emplacements, is situated on Guernsey's west coast. It was the largest batterie in the Channel Islands. The Batterie Mirus was constructed by the occupying German forces from 1941 to 1942 and was originally called Batterie Nina, named after a ship from which the guns were recovered. Later on, the name was changed to 'Mirus' in honour of Captain Rolf Mirus, who was killed in 1941 while sailing between Guernsey and Alderney. Although the guns were removed, broken up, and sold for scrap after the war had finished, the reinforced concrete structures remain intact.

The Fairy Ring, Pleinmont

The circle of stones known as the fairy ring or 'Table des Pions' can be located at the southwestern point of the island at Pleinmont. In local folklore, this site is linked with fairies, elves, and witches. However, it is said that this flat grassy area dug out of the common surrounded by a stone circle was used as a picnic bench where members of the 'Chevauchee' parade would stop and eat. The Guernsey tradition of the 'Chevauchee' was a procession that went around the island every three years checking the condition of the roads, although no one is exactly sure of the date that the 'Table des Pions' was made. It is thought to be in the late 1700s or early 1800s. The inspections of the island's roads and coastal defences were carried out by officials and Pions (footmen of the officials).

Le Catioroc (Le Trepied), St Saviour

In Guernsey folklore, the tomb was notorious as a meeting place for witches and the devil on Friday night sabbats. This site is also repeatedly mentioned in the seventeenth-century witch trials. Le Trepied is a prehistoric passage grave that was built during the Neolithic period C 4000 to 2500 BC. This site was in use until the late Bronze Age C 1000 BC. Deposited within the chamber were grave goods, including stone tools, pottery and flint, successive burials, and cremations. Its chamber is 5.5 metres long and has three surviving capstones. Le Trepied was excavated in 1840 by F C Lukis, who discovered some barbed and tanged flint arrowheads dating to C 1800 BC and some beaker-type pottery.

Fort Grey, St Pierre du Bois

Fort Grey, also known as the "Cup and Saucer" is located on a small tidal islet that is connected to the shore by a raised causeway in Rocquaine Bay on the west coast of the island. Built in 1804 as a coastal defence for protection from France, this granite tower (painted white for many years as a mariner's seamark) has a platform constructed around the tower that once carried six 24-pounder cannons. This site also served as a German anti-aircraft battery during their occupation of the island. Fort Grey was named after General Charles, Earl Grey of Howick, K.B, who was the Governor of Guernsey from 1797 to 1807. Today, Fort Grey is used as a shipwreck Museum that houses objects recovered from local wrecks, including the MV Prosperity and the Elwood Mead. Other items include a cannon from the Boreas.

Fort George, St Peter Port

Fort George, situated in St Peter Port, was a former garrison for the British Army stationed on Guernsey to defend against any French invasions during the Napoleonic wars. Construction started in 1780 and was completed in 1812; it was named after the reigning monarch, King George III. Amid the Second World War, Fort George was captured by German troops who then renamed the Fort "Base Georgefest." They built a number of gun platforms on the site and also a radar early warning station for the German Air Force. Fort George is now known as a luxury housing estate.

The Guernsey Lily (Nerine Sarniensis)

Nobody knows for sure how this beautiful flower ended up in Guernsey; the bulb originates from South Africa and is known to grow in the wild on Table Mountain and other southwestern mountains of the Cape province. Guernsey Lilies come in a variety of different colours and has been an island favourite for more than 350 years. The common belief is that the Guernsey Lily was introduced to the island when a ship sank off the west coast at Vazon on a stormy night in the mid-1800s, and the bulbs were washed ashore.

Fauxquet Valley, Castel

Fauxquet Valley's picturesque woodland walking routes takes you through a peaceful inland valley right in the heart of Guernsey, under a canopy of trees surrounding fields, ponds, and nature reserve. Whilst it has stunning scenery and views in daylight hours, dare you be brave enough to walk around the dark lanes here at night!

Castle Cornet, St Peter Port

This impressive 800-year-old castle overlooks Guernsey's capital of St Peter Port, built on a small island off the Guernsey coast to defend the Channel Islands against the French when King John lost control of Normandy in 1204, and the Channel Islands remained in possession of the English crown. The construction of the castle commenced shortly after this date.

In 1672, a lightning strike caused a fire in the castle, which destroyed Governor Lord Hatton's living quarters, the great medieval hall, and the chapel. Lord Hatton escaped death, but his wife, mother, and five other people were killed. These areas of the castle were never rebuilt.

In 1859, the castle became part of one of the breakwaters of the islands main harbour in the parish of St Peter Port.

During the German occupation on the island in World War II, Castle Cornet was taken over as the "Hafenschloss" (Harbour Castle), which was then garrisoned by an anti-aircraft unit. It had concrete gun turrets and emplacements for flak anti-aircraft guns built onto the castle's walls, as well as several concrete bunkers that were also added.

The castle has many interesting features, including several tunnels and alleys to explore, a citadel which sits at the top of the castle that can be reached via six different routes, and four beautiful period gardens within the castle walls to wander around to admire.

The museums inside the castle include a range of different artefacts and information explaining the story of Castle Cornet's history throughout the years, and at midday, the noon-day gun is fired by a 32-pounder cannon by gunners dressed in traditional 19th-century uniform.

The Vale Castle, Vale

This defensive castle stands on the hill with earthwork consisting of a ditch and bank, which was constructed back in the early Iron Age. During recent archaeological excavations at the Vale Castle, no medieval remains were found. The gatehouse and entrance of the castle are the earliest surviving parts that date back to the 15th century; the other remaining parts, such as the stone curtain walls and buttresses, were most likely built in the early 16th century.

In 1776, during the outbreak of the American war of Independence when France became an ally of the Americans causing conflict between England and France and as the Channel Islands were loyal to the English crown, this put them in danger of attacks from the French.

During 1793-1815, the time of the French Revolutionary and Napoleonic Wars, the Vale Castle was armed with one

24-pounder cannon and two nine-pounder cannons.

It was during the 1940-1945 period of the German occupation of the Channel Islands when the occupying forces demolished the derelict barracks and fortified the Vale Castle and its surrounding area. The Germans then installed extensive groundworks, which included concrete machine-gun and mortar positions, personal bunkers, and trenches. The defences that were added to the castle also featured two field guns and two searchlight positions.

Witches' Seats, West of the Island

The legendary witches' seats in the Channel Islands were built for an important purpose, according to Guernsey folklore. These small stone ledges protruding from chimneys provided a resting place for witches travelling around the island. Householders that had these built onto their homes believed that in doing so, the witches would not punish them for not providing a seat for passing witches to rest on as they flew to their sabbats.

The Devil's Hoofprint, Vale

This hoof-like indentation (Le Pied du Boeuf) situated in a rock on L'Ancresse Common derives from an old Guernsey tale where the devil was said to have left a hoofprint after being chased off the island by a saint as he leapt north in the direction of Alderney. It is said that he

214

landed on the Brayes Rocks that are situated about a mile offshore of Guernsey where hoof marks are also said to be found.

The Fairies' Bat (La Longue Rocque), St Pierre du Bois

Guernsey's largest ancient standing monument La Longue Rocque (the fairies' bat), has a visible height of 3.5 metres with a further one metre below the ground; it is estimated to weigh five tons. This tall stone menhir has a smooth worn area on the north-facing edge, possibly due to 'ritual' rubbing of the stone as some say that touching the stone increases fertility. The stone has been used as a scratching post for livestock over the 6500 years since it was set in this location.

Le Creuxes es Faies, St Pierre du Bois

This prehistoric passage tomb located on Guernsey's west coast to the north of L'Eree Bay, which is dated between 4000 to 2500 BC, was built during the Neolithic period and was in use until the late Bronze Age c 1000 BC, is known in Guernsey folklore as the entrance to the fairy kingdom.

This passage grave is nine metres long in length; the tomb entrance is narrow, which then expands further inside into a round ended chamber. Cremations and burials were deposited within the chambers of the tomb, and discoveries of grave goods, such as flint, stone tools and pottery, were also uncovered. The tomb was excavated by F C Lukis in 1840.

To the locals of Guernsey, this tomb is well known as the fairy cave; in folklore stories, it was believed that the fairies came out on moonlit nights at midnight to dance around Le Catioroc and the Mont Saint.

It has also been said that German soldiers that were barracked at L'Eree had used the tomb on occasions as a den. So, therefore, the officers in charge filled the tomb with rubble to stop this from happening. When F C Lukis started his excavations in the nineteenth century, this is how he found it. In the past, this passage tomb has even been used as a stable for Guernsey cattle.

Printed in Great Britain
by Amazon

70219954R10132